WHATEVER HAPPENED TO EVERYTHING

A Heartfelt Romantic Comedy

POPPY CARTER

ONE

New York City is peak December right now, in all its hustle–bustle festiveness, and I'm not mad about it. Serious business people and determined holiday shoppers stride through midtown, all no–nonsense as they rush through the cold clear air that whistles between the skyscrapers.

Amongst them all is a bride, almost swallowed by her huge white puff–of–cotton–candy dress, trying to get into a taxi cab. Who takes a taxi cab on their wedding day? At least get an Uber. Her bridesmaids try to push the mountain of lacy fabric through the car door, careful not to get it on the wet sidewalk –

"Emmie?"

I snap my head around, back to the boardroom with its conference table of clients. How long have they been waiting for me as I gazed out the office window at that silly bride?

"I'm sorry, I'm sorry!" Maybe if I say it twice, I'll sound more sincere.

I shuffle my papers and glance up at the power point, where was I? "You know what? I believe we can find the spirit of Christmas in FAMCO's corporate event planning."

Right about then, one of the FAMCO clients yawns, and I mean really yawns without even trying to cover it up.

But I keep going. "Yes, our work involves organizing your marketing meetings and sales conferences, but it can also unite your employees. I'd like to bring the essence of Christmas togetherness to your FAMCO events, year-round."

"Okay, Emmie – Christmas or not, tell them about the sales numbers," says Mr. M, my boss, a little impatiently. He's used to my flights of off–topic fancy, and he knows they're the reason we often land these accounts. Apparently, clients like my whimsical selling ideas, but today Mr. M's pushing me to stay on track. FAMCO is a huge account and we're all a bit nervous.

"Take a look at page three," I point to the folders in front of each of the clients. "It shows the uptick in sales after a recent motivational weekend we orchestrated – not unlike a Christmas holiday of togetherness, I might add."

Mr. M gives me a look, spinning his finger in the "keep going" motion.

So I do. "I find that creating community, whether at family holiday or a corporate weekend or perhaps even a wedding, is the absolute key to building successful sales numbers."

More is more when it comes to speaking nervously and making absolutely no sense, am I right? I keep going. "I'd like to bring the essence of the ultimate union – a wedding or a holiday – to your FAMCO events."

A couple of the FAMCO people exchange looks with tiny raised eyebrows. Is that better or worse than yawning at my presentation? Hmm, will report back.

Mr. M jumps in. "Emmie's father used to do this same job. She's a pro! It's in her blood to organize corporate events."

I smile and hope they don't sense the tiniest bit of reluctance on my part, in being defined that way. It's a lot of pressure being compared to my father, whose work was at the pinnacle of the industry. But Mr. M never misses an opportunity to make sure potential clients know I have that pedigree.

The Yawner lets loose another huge one, then announces to us that FAMCO will have to think about it.

* * *

Back at my desk, Orion is waiting. He's the most dedicated assistant a woman could have, and also makes work fun. Or as fun as it can be, I should say.

3

"Well?"

I slide into my chair and undo the updo that has been holding my hair hostage. "Well what?"

"Emmie! Did you land the account? And I'm not just asking because it affects my end-of-year bonus."

He always makes me laugh, and that keeps work bearable. "They'll let us know after Christmas, but it went okay. Fingers crossed. Now it's time for the holiday break!"

"Oh no. Here we go. I know you can't wait to switch out your high heels for ugly Christmas socks."

"I may or may not have a pair in my suitcase." I get an arched eyebrow from Orion. "Or five. And they're not ugly. They're bedazzled."

"For all those parties happening while you're in North Haven?"

"Just spending the holidays with my family. No parties."

"How about galas? Fiestas? Black–tie affairs with string quartets?"

"North Haven is more hayride than high society. But I love it."

My phone beeps a reminder at me: time to head to the train station. I stuff my laptop into the side pocket of my rolling suitcase.

Orion watches me, musing. "Just remind me real quick, when exactly are you going to tell your dad you want to be a wedding planner?"

Here we go, with our periodic sarcastic back–and–forth discussion of my life. "Uh, how about never. Because I already have a great job."

"Yeah, but Emmie, you'd be so good at–"

"At planning sales conferences and team–building corporate events."

Orion sighs in his over–the–top way. "There's a way to put your heart in your job, you know."

"My heart is with my father. I'm lucky he helped pave the way for me here, in this career. So many people would love to have this position!"

"Too bad you're not one of them." And he pulls something out. "That's why I got you some bridal magazines for the train."

Looking at the glossy covers announcing the latest bridal trends, my heart speeds up a little and I feel a lightness in my core, but I tamp it down as quickly as possible. "Why would I want those? I'm not getting married."

"Understatement alert. Especially since you don't have a boyfriend. These are for researching your new career."

"I'm happy doing corporate event planning."

"Emmie, it's me."

It's my turn for a theatrical sigh.

Orion hands them to me. "At least a side hustle?"

I grab the magazines from him. "I don't want them to go to waste."

"Merry Christmas, girlie! Now where are my ugly Christmas socks? I know you got me another pair."

He knows me too well. I pull out a gaily wrapped gift bag for him as my phone alarm tells me it's now–or–never time if I'm going to make it to the train station on time.

TWO

North Haven, Vermont is quintessential Christmas coziness in the form of a town. If you could float on your back in a cup of cocoa using a marshmallow as a raft, you would be in North Haven. Main Street has been decorated to the hilt and I'm totally here for it. All strung lights and festive happiness and white fluffy snowbanks, it's heaven in a hometown. I roll my suitcase from the train station and soak it all in. It's the greatest place on earth, for one week a year. Then I'll be ready to get back to the big city.

KTRE is the local radio station, and their studio is right on Main Street. They pipe the broadcast outside so you can hear it as you walk by, and the D.J. is visible through a window that's surrounded by Christmas lights. And that D.J. is none other than my best friend from forever and ever, Celia. I stop to watch her do her thing, smiling at her even though she hasn't see me yet.

A jingly, happy holiday carol ends and Celia speaks into the microphone. "Welcome back, listeners. This is North Haven's public radio station, KTRE. This week we've been talking to one of our newer town residents, novelist Archer Mendez."

I adjust slightly so I can see the other side of her desk. Just the back of a man is visible, his tousled brown hair and askew scarf giving him a discombobulated look. Good thing this interview isn't for TV.

I listen to them speak through the overhead speaker. "Thanks for having me today," says Archer. "I love the peace and quiet of North Haven. That's why I moved here."

Celia's smooth radio voice jumps in. "Remember, Archer is the author of the beloved *Holiday Magic*. If you've never read it, get yourself a copy."

Oh yeah, I've read that book. Now it's coming back to me – I think my mother tagged me in some neighborhood post about a writer moving to North Haven. So this must be him.

Celia continues, "And you have a long–awaited sequel in the works, I hear?"

"Yes, I do. And this new novel is quite overdue, so I'll be working straight through the holidays."

"What dedication!"

"It's more like desperation," Archer laughs.

Just then, through the window of the tiny radio station,

Celia gets a glimpse of me. She does a double take and breaks into a huge smile.

But her on–radio voice doesn't betray anything. "Archer, I hope you'll find some time for holiday fun here in North Haven?"

Archer muses, "What would be fun for me is turning this book in. But I will just take things as they come, with no set agenda. As Ralph Waldo Emerson said, 'Our painful labors are fruitless; only in our easy, simple, spontaneous action are we strong.'"

"And since we weren't all shortlisted for the Pulitzer Prize, translation please?"

Archer takes a beat, and then answers with what sounds like some real feeling. "Don't count on the future, just take life as it comes."

And on that note, Celia wraps it up and pushes a button which plays the sign–off music which ends her show. Now silently, I see her thanking Archer and gesticulating outside, pointing at me. He turns to look my way – and do I detect a grimace?

Celia bustles outside with Archer following reluctantly. Now that I can actually see him, I take in a breath. His tousled hair and askew scarf suddenly seem more male model than rumpled novelist. What is a guy this handsome doing in North Haven? I think I know why my mom sent me that link, and it wasn't because she thinks I'm a literary fan.

Celia envelops me in a hug. "Emmie, you're back!"

"Celia, I missed you so much."

She turns to include this guy whose whole demeanor says he'd rather not. "Emmie, I want you to meet someone. This is Archer Mendez, he's–"

"A novelist." I say quickly, eager to get through this conversation and release him back to the wild as soon as possible. "I heard you moved here. I read *Holiday Magic.* I loved it. So hopeful and wonderful."

Does he actually cringe at my summation of his work? "Thank you," he un–enthuses. "I wrote that book many years ago. Sometimes I think I'm not that person anymore."

"Well, I loved the kiss at the end. Happy endings are always my jam, but I actually found the positive Christmas story super believable. Realistic."

"He's writing the sequel now!" Celia says.

Archer frowns. "But it may not have the same happily ever after that you're expecting."

I'm a little taken aback by that. The *Holiday Magic* sequel might not end well? For some reason, that really upsets me.

Celia knows when to change the subject. "This is Archer's first Christmas in North Haven."

"How great. Maybe we can make a plan to show you around." That's just my politeness showing, but he counters immediately.

"I don't do plans," he says with this absolutely irritating finality.

"Excuse me?" I don't really try to keep the derision out of my voice.

Archer surprises me by laughing. "Okay, maybe that sounds ridiculous. But as soon as I make a plan to go somewhere or meet someone, I start dreading it. My favorite thing about plans is when someone else cancels them, so I don't have to."

His honesty softens me a bit. "Of course, I guess I get it."

I don't really get enjoying cancelled Christmas plans, but hey, you do you.

Celia links her arm through mine. "Archer sometimes writes at the library. He has a little place back in the corner where he hides out. Do you remember –"

"Yes! I remember we used to do our homework there in high school. I love that library. I haven't been back in years! I should go while I'm here."

Archer says, "I like the library because it's quiet. I need my privacy."

Is this guy trying to act like I'm going to stalk him or something? I feel my blood pressure rise, but not in a good way. Well maybe partially in a good way, because he's so darn cute. I hate that this is happening – my body betraying me a bit. Rude jerks should *not* be handsome.

"He has a book due soon," Celia explains.

"It's true, I have an upcoming deadline," he says. And then turns on a bit of self–effacing charm. "But I'm afraid

I'm always a bit anti–social. Hazard of the job, I guess. Ladies."

And with a proverbial tip of the hat and a smile that sends a feeling-feeling down my spine, he turns and walks away.

Celia and I look at each other. And can't help giggling, just like we've been doing since the first grade. It's wonderful to be back with my oldest friend.

THREE

Celia and I walk up to the gorgeous town Christmas tree. North Haven calls it the Wishing Tree, and it's loaded with pieces of colorful paper, each one with a handwritten wish on it, folded so no one can read it.

"The Christmas Wishing Tree never disappoints," I say. "Beautiful as ever!"

"Our whole childhood – making so many wishes here," Celia says.

We gaze up at the tree and I feel the history of our childhood Christmases warming me. "The Barbie Dream House."

"My Little Pony," she counters.

"A Furby."

"A cell phone."

"A Sephora gift card."

We laugh. "And I feel like all those wishes came true,"

I say. "Of course, our parents had a lot to do with that."

"But the Christmas Wishing Tree actually is a little magic," says Celia, gazing at the huge sparkling tree, its pine branches scattered with the hopes and dreams of townspeople.

"Come on, Celia."

"I'm serious. It's all about believing! I already made my wish, and I put it on the tree."

She turns to me expectantly.

"I think I'll wait," I say.

"I guess yours already came true, city girl!"

I nod, not even trying to be entirely convincing. "I guess so."

I take her arm and start walking around the festive town square. "I still can't believe that is the guy who wrote *Holiday Magic*. But you know what they say: never meet the artist behind your favorite things – you could be disappointed."

"I never heard anyone say that."

"Oh yeah, that's a thing."

"So you don't want to meet Taylor Swift?"

"The same rules don't apply to her."

Celia smiles. "Anyway, Archer's actually pretty nice. He was engaged once, years ago, but she passed away before they got married."

"Oooh." The air goes out of me, and empathy kicks in. That is so horrible.

Celia continues, "So maybe that's why he says he's

not as optimistic as he used to be? But he's very smart and thoughtful. And cute."

"Wait a minute. No." I know my best friend too well.

She puts on her overly innocent face. "What?"

"I just got to town. I'm literally still dragging my suitcase. And you're already fixing me up?"

"Archer is quite eligible."

"Hard no. He said himself he's anti–social. Do you even know me?"

"I just want you to have what I have," Celia's eyes fill with sincere emotion.

"Aww, Celia. How is Whit?"

"Wonderful. He's really…great."

"Okay. Your delivery could use some oomph."

She laughs. "He is great! But –"

She holds up her left hand, with its bare fingers. "He hasn't put a ring on it. And we've been dating a looooong time. I'm beginning to wonder if he wants to commit."

"Have you asked him?"

"I try to bring it up, but if I even say the word 'marriage,' he changes the subject, like he's in a panic."

I take a deep breath, and decide to give Celia my opinion. "You know, last I checked women got the vote. You could ask him. It's the 20th century."

Celia gives me the side eye. "It's the 21st century."

"Why do I always get that confused?"

"Because it's confusing. Look, I know I could ask

Whit to marry me – but first I want to ask him if I should ask him. You know?"

"Maybe Whit wants to ask you to ask him to ask you to ask him."

Celia pouts a little. "You're making fun of me."

"I am not! Okay, maybe a little." I put my arm through hers again. "But it's because I know you and Whit are made for each other. You're destined to be together."

"I hope he thinks so too."

FOUR

The house I grew up in is always decorated to the max, and this year is no exception. I love walking up and seeing it all, and knowing the joy that Mom gives us when she makes sure it's like this every year. Mom, Dad and I love the holidays and always have.

I let myself in, still pulling my suitcase. I stop to see the Christmas tree in its full glory. It may not be as big as the town Wishing Tree, but it's just as beautiful to my eyes. The holiday decorations are elaborate yet still homey.

"Mom? Dad? Ho ho ho, I'm home!"

I hear some movement in the next room, and then my parents come rushing out of the kitchen.

"Emmie! You're already here?" says my mother, Janelle.

Janelle is crafty and romantic and comforting. She's the ultimate homemaker and booboo–kisser, and I know I could not have a better mother. I also know I could never be as good at all of it as she is. Her abilities in all things homemaking are a bit intimidating. She envelops me in a minty hug.

"Smells like holiday cookies in here!" I say as I hug her back.

My businesslike and reserved father waits his turn for a hug. "So was your train early?"

"I caught the one before, I was in such a hurry to get here." I give him a hug too.

"You should've called," he says. "We could've picked you up at the station, Emmie."

"I wanted to walk through town and see the decorations up. And I stopped by and saw Celia. We went by the Christmas Wishing Tree."

"Speaking of wishes, what happened with FAMCO?" he asks.

Dad's always concerned (some might say overly invested) in everything to do with my job.

Mom shushes him. "Let her sit down first, Phil. Come have a warm cookie, Emmie."

"All I was wondering is if they liked the presentation or not."

I have to laugh. "They said they'd make their decision after Christmas. But I think they liked it, Dad. Of course it wasn't as good as you could've done."

He seems inordinately pleased with that compliment,

but he brushes it off. "Nonsense. You surpassed me years ago."

I give him another hug. "My mentor."

DING! "There's the timer!" says Mom. "Another batch of peppermint meltaways ready to go. Can you take some down to the fire station, Emmie?"

"Who's not giving her a chance to sit down now?"

Mom smiles at Dad. "I didn't mean right now…But you're right."

He softens. "I just want there to be enough cookies left for me!"

"Oh hush!"

Mom gives Dad a peck on the cheek. I have to laugh at my parents' loving back–and–forth. Some things never change. And I'm glad.

It feels great to be home for the holidays.

* * *

My childhood bedroom is a time capsule encompassing all the ups and downs of some happy growing up years. The Barbie Dream House is still in the closet, and the used–up Sephora gift card is still in the bedside table drawer. I unpack my bag and pull out the wedding magazines that Orion gave me. Flipping through, so many things catch my eye – a veil with real wildflowers laced through it, a ring with a sideways emerald–cut diamond. I'm not looking to get married, but I've always loved this stuff.

19

Which reminds me of something. I go to my closet and from the back I pull down a box of mementoes. It's one of those colorful carboard boxes, with sticker letters labeling it "MEMORIES" and a few hearts scattered around for good measure.

Among the Tamagotchis with dead batteries and dried up paint markers, I find what I'm looking for: an old notebook. On the cover in my girlish handwriting it says, "EMMIE'S PARTIES." More hearts, natch. I lift it to my face, breathing in the feel of my old childhood dreams. I get a lump in my throat – or maybe that's just the dust from all the stuff in my closet.

I make myself comfortable on the white canopy bed that I begged my parents for almost 20 years ago. My father had assured me that if they got it for me, I'd have to use it for a long, long time. Little did I know! But truth be told, I still like climbing under the white eyelet canopy and losing myself in those same dreams of my youth.

I open the notebook and look through. Photos cut from magazines of parties and weddings and showers. I made little section dividers from post–its that say things like "PARTY FAVORS" and "FUN FOOD." Honestly, this is as good as any Pinterest or inspiration board. There are a lot of great things here, perhaps even better than some of those new wedding magazines. I let myself sink into these old feelings of imagining every aspect of a great, romantic party.

Stuck into the back of the notebook I find the *piece d'*

resistance – homemade business cards, adorned with glitter markers no less. *Wedding Planner, Emmie Andrews, Age 12.* I love that I included my age, as I didn't want people to think I was too young for the job. My smile is maybe a little bittersweet as the memories of my old self keep flooding back.

"Emmie?" Mom calls from downstairs. "The cookies are all packed up!"

FIVE

Even the fire station in North Haven goes all out for the holidays, with garlands and wreaths. I take my time approaching, carrying a perfectly ribbon–wrapped plate of cookies – because Janelle never sends a holiday treat out the door with anything less than decorative perfection.

The garage door is open and firefighters mill about, playing cards or reading. I know most of them, okay all of them – but one is a bestie.

"Emmie! You're back in town!"

"Whit!" I'm so happy to see him. Not only is he the boyfriend of Celia, but he's just an all–around great guy.

Whit takes the plate of cookies. "Your mom's peppermint meltaways?"

"You know it."

"Celia is going to be so excited to see you–"

"I already stopped by the radio station."

Whit is uncharacteristically nervous all of the sudden. "You did? What did she say?"

"Um, just the usual. We talked about, let's see –"

A couple of other firefighters walk up so Whit interrupts me. "Here gentleman! Mrs. Andres' famous Christmas cookies."

As the firefighters take the plate and dig in, Whit pulls me aside nervously.

"Well? What did Celia say?"

Now I'm getting a little worried. "Whit, what is going on?"

He glances back at his co–workers. "Come on." He leads me down the street.

The best bakery in town is called Cake My Day, and that's exactly where Whit's taking me.

"The peppermint meltaways weren't good enough for you?" I kid Whit.

He grabs a couple of hot cocoas for us, and hustles me toward a table away from the few other patrons. As we sit down, my curiosity gets the better of me. "Whit, seriously – is everything okay?"

"Emmie, I have to ask you something. Very seriously. I need your help."

I'm concerned, and I want to be there for my friend. "Of course."

He fidgets nervously, and takes a deep breath. "The thing is… Well, I'm going to propose to Celia on Christmas Eve."

"That's wonderful!!"

He glances around and shushes me. "I want it to be a surprise," he practically whispers. "Actually, I want it to be a surprise party."

If I knew what swooning was, I would do it right now. "How incredibly fun!"

"And not only a surprise party, but I have this crazy idea…" he stops, looking sheepish.

"Whit, come on! Crazy ideas are kind of my thing! Spill it."

"I was imagining a whole week of perfect holiday activities leading up to the surprise party. You know how much Celia loves Christmas."

"Almost as much as me."

"Exactly. I just want it to be a really, really fun week for her. Kind of like, the best week of her life?"

"No pressure," I laugh.

"Yeah, right. I mean, there's no way I could pull it off. Unless maybe – Emmie, could you help me with all of this?" I take in his sweet, desperate puppy dog face.

"Hmm, let's see. Can I plan a surprise party for my best friend to get engaged on Christmas Eve, along with a week of fun holiday activities leading up to it?" I pretend to give the entire request some serious consideration. "I mean – have you ever heard so many great words stuffed into one sentence? Twist my arm! I'm in!"

Whit's relief is palpable. "Thanks so much, Em. You're the best."

Minutes later, I am still bubbling over with ideas, in between sweet sips of Cake My Day's incredibly good cocoa. "Another idea is to have it in a hotel ballroom, and do a sort of royal theme. Celia and I used to love Cinderella – we could do that theme, but with a Christmas twist. Maybe instead of a pumpkin turning into a carriage, it could be a cranberry?"

Whit's cocoa is long gone, and he looks a little dazed. "I love your enthusiasm, but my head is spinning."

"Speaking of spinning – we'll definitely need music. You know what, we should think about a live band. Or is a D.J. better?"

Whit glances over my shoulder. "Archer! There you are."

I freeze. This is harshing my buzz. Mr. I Don't Like Plans is about to butt into my planning session. I turn slowly, carefully arranging my face into a noncommittal half smile.

Whit is now energized though. "Archer, I want you to meet Emmie."

"Ah yes, the person who still believes in *Holiday Magic*." On the one hand, Archer's smile looks genuine, but also he is clearly making fun of me.

"If it isn't the anti–social novelist who just moved to town."

We exchange wary smiles, and I can tell Whit is not sure what to make of all this. "So you've met."

Archer pulls out a chair. "May I?"

25

"Actually, we're sort of in the middle of something," I tell him.

"Oh, I asked Archer to come here today. To help."

I look at Whit like he's crazy, because how is this guy going to help. "You did?"

Archer goes ahead and takes a seat. He seems to be enjoying this mix–up. "Whit and I were college roommates. He's a big reason I moved here." The two guys share a meaningful glance – they're clearly old buddies. I sense a history there.

Whit charges on, sensing I still need some convincing. "Emmie, you know this whole week of activities and the party and everything? Well it would just mean so much if all four of us could be involved. My old friend, Archer. And Celia's old friend, Emmie."

"Of course, everyone's invited," I say.

But that's not exactly what Whit meant. "I was kind of hoping the two of you could work together to make this happen and figure out what to do. It would be like a combination of my past and Celia's past, coming together. Both our voices heard and represented."

I'm touched. "Which is exactly what a marriage should be…"

Archer clears his throat. I sense he's not into this touchy–feely stuff.

"So will you two do it?" Whit asks.

Archer and I turn to look at each other. That hair of his is still messy, and I notice his eyes are a hazel green color with gold flecks. The height of annoyingly classic good looks.

"Well?" Whit asks.

Archer and I snap our gazes back toward Whit, realizing we just held each other's eye for a tiny beat too long.

My "Of course we will!" is overlaid with Archer's simultaneous "No problem!"

Whit doesn't seem entirely convinced, but he takes our word for it. "Great!"

"Great," I say.

"Great," Archer says.

It is so *not* great.

SIX

Archer and I walk Whit back to work at the fire station. Whit takes the opportunity to thank his old friend.

"I really appreciate you agreeing to this, Archer."

"Honestly, I don't know how helpful I'll be."

"It'll be nice to have you there to kind of represent the man's point of view. Besides, maybe it'll help you too?"

"That sounds a little self–serving."

I wonder what he means by that, but I don't interrupt.

Whit continues, "Hey, we all get to hang out, and I get to pop the question to Celia – it's a win–win!"

Archer is a bit less enthusiastic. "What I need to do is get over my writer's block, not plan parties!" The guys share a laugh.

Whit's feeling a bit sentimental. "The four of us together having fun – this is going to be the best week of Celia's life! And mine too."

Whit waves goodbye as he goes into the fire station.

"No pressure," I say.

"None at all."

So…awkwardness descends. Archer breaks it first, "Which way are you going?"

I point.

"Me too. To the library." He seems resigned as he asks, "Shall we walk together so we can talk about all this ensuing holiday merriment?"

"Absolutely." I can't help it, even if Archer is ho–hum about all of this, I feel totally invigorated by the possibilities. As we walk the holiday–decorated streets of North Haven, the spirit of love and Christmas inspires me more and more.

"We'll make sure every detail is personalized. The most important thing is to absolutely overload us on all things Christmas cheer!"

Archer offers a stage whisper to the skies: "Help."

I give him a frown and slow down. "Excuse me?"

"I'm sorry, I'm sorry. Go ahead, you were saying – Christmas cheer overload?"

"Our first order of business should really be a venue for the party. I have a couple of ideas. Christmas Eve is only one week away. There are so many preparations to be made."

"We should be able to throw something decent together in a week."

"The verb 'throw together' is not how I roll, nor is the

adjective 'decent.' Now we need to think about food, decorations, a photographer."

"A nice, quiet place."

"A fun, festive place! Maybe a videographer in addition to the photographer? Of course music, party favors, centerpieces."

"This is for the proposal, right? Not a royal wedding."

"What do you think of a slideshow of their whole relationship?"

"Sounds a bit overdone."

"It will be wonderful! We'll set the stage for their magical moment."

"Magical moments mustn't be manufactured." He looks proud of his alliteration.

"But beautiful blessings are best built."

Archer can't help smiling at my response. "Respect," he tells me.

And I feel that smile in my bones. I shake it off and continue. "Then there are the daily fun activities. I was thinking we could do a Christmas movie night, but personalized with all of Whit and Celia's favorite holiday movie moments?"

"Or we can can just see what's on TV that night."

I try to ignore that idea. "One day, maybe all of us can go sledding, then have a winter picnic of their favorite foods?"

Archer heaves a sigh.

"What??"

Archer stops and turns to me, no longer smiling. "Doesn't all of this planning create a sort of contrived, overdone atmosphere? Who has fun like that?"

"I do."

SEVEN

As we arrive at my family home, I feel a tiny tinge of embarrassment at all the decorations. Knowing how Archer feels about over–the–top celebrations, I'm suddenly self-conscious.

"This is my parents' place," I tell him.

"I thought it was Santa's Workshop."

"Thank you. Even though I know you meant that in a completely condescending way."

Archer laughs. We pause to say goodbye, and for some reason there are butterflies in my belly. I guess I'm just really excited about planning all this holiday fun.

"Emmie, seriously – how are we going to keep the proposal a surprise party? Isn't Celia going to be a little suspicious about us doing all of these Christmas things?"

"Believe it or not, some of us make a lot of holiday

plans every year. The only suspicious part might be you joining in."

"Touché. I just think –"

Right then I have a lightbulb moment and interrupt him. "Oh! What about holiday bowling? And we could wear Christmas light–up necklaces?"

"Look Emmie, I can see you are really into all of this holiday–" He uses his fingers to bracket the word "fun."

"Please do not use air quotes when referring to Christmas joy."

He smiles at me again, and I really hate how susceptible I am to those crinkles around his eyes when he does. "Sorry, Emmie."

"Nothing to be sorry about. I'm not mad, there are just some fundamental differences of opinion here."

"Exactly. I gotta be honest. I just don't think planning out every detail of what is *supposed* to happen does any good."

"Of course it does!"

A darkness flits across Archer's face. "It certainly doesn't guarantee happiness. No matter what you plan, it could all fall apart. In an instant."

I realize what he's talking about and I feel like a completely ditzy fool. Talking about parties and fun, when he's suffered past loss. "Oh right."

Maybe Archer realizes he's revealed himself accidentally, because he gets flustered. "Anyway, you seem to love all this silly party stuff. So why don't you do it with them?"

Now it's my turn to be flustered. "We told Whit we'd do it together."

"I'll tell him I'm busy with my book deadline. He'll understand."

"...Okay." I feel bad now. Have I been too hard on him, and pushed him out of having fun with us? He starts to turn away so I throw out: "Would you like to come in for one of my mom's Christmas cookies? They're kind of famous. In North Haven, at least."

He looks genuinely surprised, and maybe even touched. But that pain skitters around his face again and he just says, "I'll pass. Have a nice evening."

He turns and walks away. I want to say something but I can't tell if he just insulted me, or he's mad because I insulted him or what just happened. So I settle on, "Merry Christmas!"

Archer doesn't turn around, doesn't even respond.

How rude is that?

EIGHT

I sit at the kitchen island watching as Mom frosts and decorates a yule log. She's actually including little marzipan toadstools and the whole thing is too cute for words.

But I'm very busy ranting about this so–called novelist in town. "The whole point is to build a sort of shared experience of having fun, where Archer says what Whit would like and I say what Celia would like, and together we make sure we've arranged something that's fun for both of them. But he's being impossible. He just gave up and quit!"

Mom goes to the fridge door and pulls down a photo.

I continue, "Should I just tell Whit it's not going to work out? Or should I go ahead and do it all myself, for the three of us?"

"No."

I'm confused. "No to which?"

"Both." Mom hands me an old snapshot off the refrigerator: It's me and Celia approximately a thousand years ago, showing off our ugly Christmas socks and mouths full of braces.

"The Santa Soiree! That was so fun."

"You arranged it all, Emmie. The decorations, food, everything. But that's not what made it fun."

"Thanks a lot, Mom."

She chuckles. "What made it fun was all the people who came." She gazes at me in a very mother–knows–best angelic way.

"I know you're sending me some sort of coded holiday lesson here, but what is it?

She laughs, but remains earnest. "The important thing to Celia and to Whit is that they're with friends. You have to make sure this Archer fellow is part of the fun."

I take a deep breath. "How are you always right?"

"I went to Mom School, of course. Top of my class."

"*Summa cum laude* in baking, for sure. Not to mention decorating and entertaining."

"Apple doesn't fall too far from the Christmas tree," and she gives me a wink.

For some reason, that feels like the best compliment I've ever gotten. "I love you, Mom." I grab another cookie. "And it's not just because of your peppermint meltaways."

She laughs as I take a bite. "But it doesn't hurt!"

I sit enjoying the cookie, but Mom gives me a look.

"What?"

She motions her head toward the door.

"You mean I should go –"

"Yes."

"To talk to –"

"Yes."

"Now?"

"You have an hour before dinner. Go."

NINE

The North Haven Library is another classic village building that's been decorated to the utmost. There are signs about Christmas storytimes and Christmas book club meetings and Christmas hours and even the upcoming Christmas Wishing Tree lighting ceremony. I'm thinking this is a funny place to work for a guy who doesn't believe in happy endings.

I charge inside and am immediately taken with the smell and feel of this sacred, happy building of books. I'm transported back to high school, when Celia and I would hang out and talk more than we studied, buried in the stacks. I love this place. I walk the aisles, almost forgetting why I'm there. I wave to a couple of people I've known all my life and slow down, taking it all in.

I realize I'm in the fiction aisle, under the letter M. I run my finger along the spines of the books until I come to a well–worn volume, *Holiday Magic* by Archer Mendez. No one's around, so I pull it off the shelf. "The Most Hopeful Book of the Holiday Season" reads the blurb on the cover. I open to the inside book–jacket and there's a photo of Archer, from several years ago. Why look at that, he'd actually combed his hair. I think I like it better messy. But his eyes were still that same variation of golden sparkles embedded in green.

"Emmie?"

I slam the book shut and thrust it behind my back. Because of course you know who just said my name.

"Hey Archer. What are you doing here?" I'm good at a lot of things, but playing it cool and keeping a secret are not among them.

Archer on the other hand, seems as relaxed and amused as can be. "You know what's great? That you don't seem awkward or embarrassed at all right now."

"Why would I be embarrassed?"

"Maybe because you're holding my book behind your back?"

I sag. I'm caught. "I happened to walk by it on the shelf –"

"Way back here?" His tone is teasing, his smile and arched eyebrow pronounced.

"Okay. I was back in this corner because actually I was looking for you. Archer, we have to work together to make this week great for Whit and Celia. She's my best friend. And you're Whit's best friend. And – and –"

I forget what I am about to say as Archer takes a step toward me, never breaking eye contact. He reaches around behind me and pulls my hand forward, with his book still in it. He gingerly, tenderly even, opens the book to where my finger is still inserted – right on his author photo.

My embarrassment is big, but I'm not sure that is what's making me feel so hot and shaky right now. Archer has his hand on mine, as we both look down at the book now. A long quiet moment standing together among the stacks of books, a faint Christmas carol over the muzak speakers. We're all alone.

Finally he says, "I went through a rough time and Whit was there for me. We hadn't seen each other since college – but he reached out. And so yes, it's important to me too. I want to make this really special for them. Even if that means…" He finally looks back up into my eyes, just a foot away. "Making plans."

He shudders and pulls the book out of my hands. I fake-chuckle as I try to make my heart beat slower. Archer shelves the book and says to me, "Let's do this."

I look right into his eyes and say, "It will be-" and I cup my fingers around the word "fun."

He laughs and for some reason that laugh makes me laugh. My enthusiasm is back. "Here's to the most romantic week of Christmas activities ever! Tomorrow, first up is sleigh ride caroling."

"I'm almost afraid to ask."

TEN

It's the mid-morning rush at Cake My Day, which means a couple dozen friendly townspeople are all sitting around talking about their nearest and dearest, as they snack on flaky holiday pastries and glorious caffeinated concoctions. Life is good at the cutest little Christmas-y bakery in North Haven, Vermont.

I'm sitting alone in the back though, engrossed in making notes about the upcoming surprise party. Of course I also have a hot cocoa and a candy cane croissant. I'm not a monster.

Archer walks up, his own bakery cardboard cup in hand. "Elf reporting for duty."

"Where's your pointy green hat?"

He slides into the chair next to me, instead of the one across the table. "At the cleaners. At least I have a hot chocolate."

"It's hot cocoa."

Archer tilts his head. "Is there a difference?"

I recoil in mock horror. "You definitely have not achieved elf status.

He throws up his hands, with a smile. "So what's the…"

I lean forward, waiting. "Come on you can do it."

He gives me a get-off-my-back grin.

"Plan," I enunciate. "Come on, you can say it."

"What arrangements need to be completed in order to organize the upcoming occurrence?"

"Because that's so much easier than 'plan.'" I turn my old notebook toward him. I added some pages last night. I show him the one labeled *Sleigh Ride Caroling* – "Tonight will be Sleigh Ride Caroling."

"You don't say."

I roll my eyes and flip to the next page, where I've pasted inspo photos and sketched out some ideas, all rather artfully done if I do say so myself.

"You did this?!"

"Just some notes." Why do I feel the heat rising in my cheeks? These are just party ideas. Who cares what he thinks anyway? Obviously I do, for some insane reason. I continue, "So the idea is a horse-drawn sleigh, but there's not enough snow on the actual streets to accommodate that, so a horse drawn carriage will work."

Archer impersonates a horse, "Neigh!"

"I'm ignoring that remark. We'll decorate the carriage

with garlands and lights, and have thermoses of hot chocolate-"

"You mean hot cocoa."

"In the evening? What are we, amateurs?"

"Just testing you."

"Then we ride around to houses and sing Christmas carols!"

Archer looks over the plan for a few long, silent seconds. "I hope the horse is strong enough."

"For what?"

"To carry a tune."

ELEVEN

I brought the garlands and ornaments with me, so we're able to go decorate the carriage in advance. Archer's not exactly enthusiastic, but he's not a grinch either. In fact, I kind of like the way he's twisting the greenery around the edge of the carriage seat, but I don't tell him that.

"Oh, I got us an appointment for tomorrow to look at the party space behind Kat's, which is a-"

"A restaurant on the edge of town," he says. "I know it well."

"How long have you been here?"

"Just under a year. And you know what? I really love it."

"You sound surprised," I tease.

"I thought it was a temporary thing, for sure. But it feels good here. What made you move away?"

"Bright lights, big city, glamorous opportunities. To

work sixty hour weeks and deal with crowds and insane rents." I chuckle. "I sound so negative. New York is a fantastic place."

"It is. I mean, I lived in Brooklyn for years and loved it. But it was time for a change."

Archer's mood darkens a bit, and it feels like a weighty pause. So I try to change the subject as I affix battery-operated Christmas lights to the carriage.

"Well, it would be great if we could get this room at Kat's for the party. She just had a cancellation, which often happens around the holidays, surprisingly. A lot of moving parts to holiday gatherings."

"Whit said you do this sort of stuff for a living?"

"Well, I do corporate events, sales conventions, HR training sessions and the like."

"But those don't have-" He motions toward my notebook. "Decorations and themed snacks."

"More like power points and breakout sessions. The real world."

Archer wrangles a garland into place. "So how'd you get into that?"

"My father. He taught me everything, and I followed in his footsteps. It's a real growth industry. There's so much room for advancement."

"Sounds secure," Archer said, but there is a question under that statement that bothers me.

"We're vying for a huge new account, and I should

know soon if we get it. If we do,'" I cross my fingers. "It could mean years of steady work. I'm very lucky."

"So you have it all *planned* out?"

I throw a stray holly berry off the garland, hitting him in the chest. "That's me. The planner. The corporate events planner."

"I guess I just assumed your career would have something to do with, I don't know, glitter and hors d'oeuvres?"

"They're called appetizers these days. And glitter is environmentally dangerous."

"What? I found a Christmas décor you don't like?"

"Oh, I just mix food coloring with salt. It's safe, nontoxic, and looks even more sparkly than real glitter."

"Can't keep a holiday decorator down." He smiles at me. Like, *smiles* at me.

I step away, deep breath, and take a critical eye toward the carriage we've been decorating. "Perfect. And by perfect, I mean it'll do."

We both reach down at the same time to gather the remaining unused decorations. It's a face-to-face moment, and although it's awkward, we both freeze for a beat. It's the weirdest thing – almost feels like an attraction. Because of course it is an attraction – between two people who are absolutely wrong for each other. As if both of us realize that at the same moment, we stand in unison.

"So uh, what else should I do for tonight?" he asks the ground.

46

"Could you bring a couple of blankets?"

"Sure."

"Do you have any reindeer antlers that we could all wear? The inflatable ones are fine."

"Do I look like someone with four sets of reindeer antlers lying around?"

"I mean, I figured you were good for at least three."

As we exchange wry smiles, Archer's phone buzzes. He pulls it out of his pocket, and without meaning to, I look at the screen and see that "Maude" is calling.

"My agent," he moans.

"Well, I'll let you go. I've got to get home."

"I'm walking that way too. Mind if I tag along?"

"Uh, no."

And so Archer answers his facetime, and talks to his agent as he walks alongside me. It's impossible not to listen, so even though I don't want to be nosy, I of course do want to be nosy. And I hang on every word, curious about the career details of this pretty-famous novelist.

"Hey, Maude."

"Archer, my treasured and amazing client, how ARE you?" I catch a sideways glimpse of Maude, and she's probably in her 70s and sitting in a glamorous wood-paneled office.

"It's going, um, okay. Still a little stuck on that last scene."

"You'll figure it out, with your talent."

"Luckily the January 1 deadline is two weeks away, so-"

"That's why I called you, you skilled scribe."

"Every compliment makes me more nervous."

Maude laughs, then gets down to brass tacks. "The editor leaves for her vacation on December 24. She's going on a safari."

"Who goes on safari for Christmas?" Archer wonders.

"Very elite literary publishing house employees. And while said editor is on a 27-hour flight to the continent of Africa, she'd like to be reading her most anticipated new title for next year."

I can feel the panic wash over Archer. "I'm sure you're not saying the book is due on Christmas Eve."

"Oh no. I was going to say the manuscript is due on December 24."

"Maude!"

I honestly feel like I'm eavesdropping at this point, but when I speed up my gait, Archer matches it.

"Look, you already know what the ending is, right?"

"I'm researching, but it's tricky."

Maude becomes gentle with him. "I know it's difficult for you to go back and write about Christmas joy again. But you have to find your mojo, Archer."

He glances sideways at me. Finally feeling a bit self-conscious. "I'll try."

Before Maude hangs up, she re-affirms: "No matter what, it's due at midnight on December 24!"

TWELVE

I'm in the kitchen, packing up snacks for tonight. As I tie red and green ribbon around each bag of caramel corn, I can't help thinking about Archer's new deadline. I told him he should stay home and work tonight, but he wouldn't hear of it.

I check the "Sleigh Ride Caroling" page of my notebook. Almost everything is now checked off. Oh yeah, cinnamon sticks to stir the hot cocoa. I go to the spice cabinet to find some, just as Dad breezes in.

"Did you hear yet if you got it?" he asks.

His bright enthusiasm is met with my distracted smile. "We don't tour Kat's restaurant until tomorrow."

"Kat's? Emmie, I'm talking about-"

I suddenly realize what he means. "Oh sorry, the FAMCO account! No, haven't heard yet." I wave my crossed fingers and give him a big smile.

"I know you've got this. Emmie, FAMCO is a career-defining opportunity."

"I know, Dad. It's the dream." I give him a heartfelt smile and start tucking the snacks into a little picnic basket that I lined with red and green patterned napkins.

"What's all this, Emmie-lu?"

I realize he's noticed my notebook, and I move to close it but he stops me. "Oh nothing. Just going out with Celia and the gang tonight.

Dad looks over the page carefully, which makes me squirm a little. All the sudden I'm ten and he's looking over a B+ on my report card. Andrews always make straight As, don't you know.

"This sure is detailed, Em."

"Ha! I was just playing around." I push forward and grab the notebook, closing it. "I have to go shower for tonight. Love, you, Dad." And I kiss him on the way out of the kitchen.

* * *

Main Street of North Haven is always gorgeous, but never more so than when the sparkly Christmas lights are strung across it, with ribbons and garlands wrapping the lamp poles. I stand by the horse and carriage, under the starry clear sky of a beautiful Vermont night. Archer's nearby, but he hasn't said much as we wait for Celia and Whit to arrive. And here they come now.

"What is all of this!" squeals Celia.

"Just felt like having some fun!" I tell her. Whit gives me a wink behind Celia's back.

She oohs and ahs at the decorated carriage. "Just like the old days, when you used to organize all sorts of crazy Christmas stuff."

I feel Archer glance toward me, wondering. But I ignore it. "I still dabble occasionally. You first."

As Celia and Whit get in the carriage, Archer catches Emmie's eye.

"Well?" I ask him, quietly.

"Well what?"

"Well, looks like the *plan* is actually going to be fun?"

He smiles. Just as Archer is about to admit defeat, ACHOO! Whit sneezes. And then sneezes twice more.

Archer says, "You getting a cold, pal?"

"No, no, I'm fine." ACHOO!

We ride in the carriage through the cold, clear night, looking at the beautiful lights, talking and laughing amidst Whit's occasional sneezes. I reach down and dole out cups of hot chocolate from the thermos.

Archer raises an eyebrow at me: "No marshmallows."

But I whip out some marshmallows, with a triumphant smile. The look on his face says: you win. Just then, the carriage goes over a pothole, and we all spill hot chocolate everywhere.

"It's all over the blankets!" says Celia. "I'm so sorry."

"No worries at all," Archer assures her.

Trying to distract and keep the caroling ball rolling, I say, "Our first house is right up here!"

The carriage pulls up to an adorable Craftsman house, complete with wreaths in every window and ornate lights on every curve of the roof. Archer starts to climb down.

"Wait, what are you doing?" I ask. "We stay in here. This is sleigh ride caroling."

Whit glances over the side of the carriage. "Is this a sleigh?"

"A carriage, you know what I mean." A bit flustered, I ring some sleigh-bells that I brought.

The four of us sit, waiting. I ring the sleigh-bells again, louder…

"Should I go ring the doorbell?" Celia offers.

"No! I mean, that's okay." I ring the bells a third time, and someone passing a window inside the house glances out. I wave frantically to get their attention.

All of this is amusing Archer.

The family who lives in this adorable house gathers around their door, almost filling the porch. They wait expectantly, smiling.

I pull a pitch pipe out of my jacket, blow a note, and the four of us burst into *Jingle Bells*. We are really putting our hearts into the singing, but it's punctuated by Whit's sneezing. We keep on singing though.

The Grandma on the porch asks loudly, "Are they going to sing?"

The teenager standing next to her says, "They are singing, Grandma."

"Well, I can't hear them!"

The four of us try to sing even louder. Which makes Whit sneeze again.

"I think I'm allergic to horses," he admits.

THIRTEEN

Celia and Whit say their goodbyes, as Archer and I gather the basket and food out of the carriage.

"That was really fun," says Celia as she hugs me goodnight.

"Fun as in disastrous?"

Archer chimes in. "We'll make it up to you. Why don't we do something else tomorrow night?"

I'm absolutely shocked that Archer offered this up, but I try to act natural. "Yeah, that sounds like a good idea."

Whit chimes in, and he's maybe a worse faker than even me. "That would be great! Yeah, let's do something else tomorrow."

"Wonderful." Archer nods and gives me a wink.

But Celia notices. She gives me a look that can only pass between old friends, which means: *I think Archer likes you!!*

And I return it with a look which means: *Absolutely not.*

* * *

Celia and Whit are long gone by the time Archer and I take the last of the decorations off the carriage and wave goodnight to the driver.

"Well," says Archer. He looks like he wants to laugh.

"Go ahead."

"Go ahead with what?" His mock innocence is killing me. I roll my eyes.

"Emmie, surely you don't think that I'm the type of person to say, 'I told you so'?"

I shake my head and cross my arms, steeling myself for the ribbing that's coming my way.

"I mean, come on Emmie. Would I really rub your face in this calamity of a *planned* Christmas activity? Would I point out that it was freezing tonight, no one could hear us singing, Whit is allergic to horses, and Celia spent the whole night covered in hot cocoa-soaked pants?"

"Hot chocolate."

"Exactly. I'd never say all of that."

I have to laugh too. "What a night! Well, I can't wait to see what you come up with."

Archer stops laughing. "Um, what?:

"We're both doing this, right? Aren't you the one who told them we'd be doing something tomorrow?"

55

"That's when I assumed you would be handling it."

My triumphant smile returns.

"I'll see you at Kat's tomorrow morning to tour the party venue. I'm sure by then, you'll have the upcoming occurrence all organized and arranged."

* * *

The next morning, Archer and I are being shown around the party room at Kat's by none other than Kat herself. She's in her forties, a cheery saleswoman who always seems to be in a hurry. The place is plenty big enough, and has the beginnings of some nice Christmas decorations.

"We'll be able to bring in more Christmas lights, right?" I ask Kat.

"More?" says Archer.

"And one big Christmas tree here, then a few others scattered about." I am starting to picture it all. "Lots of garlands across this back wall, framing the windows."

Archer ignores all of that, and asks Kat, "Could we hear the sound system?"

Kat goes off to oblige.

"So Archer, what do you hink? Tinsel across this whole area, and more lights?"

"I'm suddenly remembering the term 'Christmas cheer overload' being bandied about."

"Exactly! It will be amazing."

Archer slides his foot across the hardwoods. "Seems like a good dance floor."

"Hmm, dance floor? Not sure we need that. Probably put more tables right there."

"What! Dancing is the main event of any great party."

"Says the man who considers himself anti-social."

"Yes, but I've read a lot. And in books people always dance. Besides, Whit and Celia love it."

He has me there. The music comes over the sound system, and wouldn't you know it's Taylor Swift. One of her slow songs, nice and romantic.

"Great sound system," Archer says. He motions his head slightly, as if asking me to dance.

"No thank you." I pull out my notebook, with today's list. "We need to meet with the chef. And check the electrical grid to see if it will support more lights."

"Be spontaneous. Do something not on the list." He reaches out, inviting me onto the dance floor.

"Are you literally just doing this to bug me right now?"

"We have to check the dance floor. Any responsible party planner would do that."

Right on cue the overheads dim and Christmas lights send sparkles into a disco ball, the whole room turning to holiday magic. It just got real romantic.

"Kat's giving us the full treatment, I guess," I say, shrugging.

"You're telling me sleigh ride caroling is a thing, but dancing is not? Come on."

I find his mischievous grin a little bit cute. Sue me.

I offer my hand, and Archer pulls me out onto the dance floor as TSwift talks about her lover, lover. Why am I so surprised that Archer is an assured dancer? We are barely touching, just the gentle pressure of his hand on my back with my hand lightly on his shoulder – but the crackle of attraction is there. At least on my end, he's probably not thinking that at all.

"Beautiful," says Archer.

He's looking at me but he's talking about the room. "Yeah, this dance floor seems fine."

Is he holding me a little closer now, or is that just my imagination?

"Emmie?" he half-whispers.

This moment of eye contact keeps going, sparking back and forth between us. I suddenly imagine kissing him and so I repeat over and over in my mind "Don't think about kissing Archer!" and you can imagine how well that goes.

"Yes, Archer?" I whisper back.

"You're…an okay dancer."

How does he keep making me laugh?

Abruptly, the lights turn on and the music comes to a halt, just as Taylor is singing you're-my-my-my…lover. I practically jump out of Archer's arms, and turn to Kat.

I babble, "It's great. We'd love to reserve the room for Christmas Eve. Thank you so much. We'll take it."

FOURTEEN

As Archer and I leave the restaurant, we pull on our gloves and hats against the brisk and beautiful winter weather. I try to play it cool: like, dancing? What dancing?

"So tonight, we're - ?" I give him a questioning look.

"Meeting at Tinsel Corners, by the Wishing Tree."

"And then?" He doesn't fill in, so I prod. "We'll go do something?"

Archer has a twinkle in his eye. I think he enjoys stringing me along. Kind of like a best friend's big brother or something. He just enjoys teasing me. That dance meant nothing, I tell myself.

"That's right," says Archer. "We'll be doing something not in your notebook. See you then."

And with a sly smile, he gets in his car and leaves.

How could I have been even slightly, remotely attracted to this guy? What a jerk.

At home, Mom needs help decorating some spangled Christmas socks, and I'm happy to oblige. It's been years since I sewed on sequins and drew designs with puffy paint. The socks are gloriously gaudy and ugly, but we are having lots of fun. But I do find myself giving her the latest on Archer.

"He's so annoying, and it's like it's just done specifically to bother me."

She gives me a knowing, amused smile.

"Don't," I say.

All innocence: "Whatever do you mean?"

"This is not one of those enemy to love things where I suddenly go, 'Actually he's great and he was right in front of my face the whole time!' This guy is actively trying to irritate me, Mom. He won't tell me what we're doing tonight. Why not? Christmas is about making plans. How am I supposed to make sure everything goes well?"

"Maybe just trust him a little."

I barely have time to roll my eyes at that before my phone rings. It's Mr. M via video chat.

I tell Mom, "Maybe he already heard back from FAMCO!"

I hustle out onto the back porch, slipping on my coat as I answer the FaceTime. "Mr. M! Merry Christmas! How are you?"

As usual, he's straight to business. "Did you get my email?"

"Oh, no. When did you send it?"

"Two minutes ago. It's about FAMCO."

I'm feeling hopeful, excited, nervous. "Yes?"

"No word on whether we got the account. But they're having an emergency merger negotiations meeting on December 24. Top secret, last-minute thing. They have to make the deal before the end of this calendar year."

"I see," I said. Even though I did not see.

"I told them you could do it, of course."

Uh oh. I hesitate, as a hundred questions flash through my mind. "What do they need?"

"Great. Thanks."

"Well, I'm not sure- I mean, maybe I could work remotely."

"Book a place, make the arrangements. It's all in the email I sent you. Make sure and check your email regularly, Emmie."

"I will."

"This is good news, Em. It could be the tipping point. We do this right, the entire international account could be ours."

I take this in. I mean, wow. That seriously is a huge opportunity.

"I'll get right on it."

* * *

After an entire afternoon sending emails and making transatlantic reservations, I am feeling pretty spent. It's a

61

good thing it wasn't my job to arrange today's activity. I meet Celia and Whit at the Christmas Wishing Tree, which is now loaded with even more pieces of colorful paper, each one with a handwritten wish on it.

"Em, have you made your wish yet?" Celia asks.

"Not yet."

"It's a tradition. And yours always come true."

I don't know how to explain why I haven't made a Christmas wish yet – maybe it's because I'm not entirely sure what to wish for. Oh to be back in the days where an American Girl doll could solve all your problems. But before I can explain some version of that to Celia, Archer shows up.

"Hey everybody!" He seems cheerful.

"There you are," says Celia.

"Hey man," says Whit.

"Hi Archer," I offer.

And then we just stand there looking at each other. Waiting. Archer just smiles at each of us in turn, looking totally relaxed. He even whistles a Christmas carol at one point.

Finally, I can't stand it any longer. "Well?"

"Is a hole in the ground," he offers.

"Are you enjoying your dad humor?" I ask him.

"Yes, thank you."

Whit laughs, and so does Celia. But I just can't find it funny, after the busy day I've had. "So what are we doing here, Archer?" I demand.

"I just thought it would be fun for the four of us to hang out."

Whit chimes in, "Absolutely!"

But I keep pushing. "Why here though? What do you have planned?" I'm on the edge of my seat waiting to hear the answer.

Archer looks into my eyes for a long second, which I feel all the way into my toes. And finally he answers: "Nothing. I have nothing planned."

"Nothing at all?"

There goes that smile of his again. "Let's just see what happens."

By now, I'm huffing around like a holiday grump. "Well, it's North Haven on a Tuesday. I'm guessing not much!"

Celia must be a little mortified by my tantrum, because she says, "All good though."

A beat as the four of us just stand around. Archer seems calm, fine to do nothing. But I can't help it, I immediately go into helpful Elf mode.

"You know we could go have a Christmas movie night at my parents' house," I offer.

Archer notices something. "Wait, what's this?"

We all turn to see a passenger van pulling up. Painted on the side is "North Haven Retirement Community." The van has a red nose and antlers on the hood, with holiday lights around the antenna.

"You mean the retirement home residents? They're probably coming to do some Christmas shopping," I say.

"Perfect!" Archer replies.

Even Celia and Whit exchange a skeptical look.

"Perfect what?" I ask.

"We'll go shopping with them."

* * *

Soon, Whit and Celia have paired off with a gentleman named Willie who is a retired farmer. I find myself with Archer and a retirement home patron named Gail, who's in her 80s and quite flamboyant. He offers her his arm, and heads slowly toward a nearby gift shop. I lag behind, listening to Gail and Archer chatting.

"I can do all my shopping at the boutique," Gail says. "Just need something for my daughter and two granddaughters."

"We're happy to tag along and assist, if you don't mind," says Archer.

"Honey, you carry the packages and open the doors, I'll shop with you all day long."

"Alright then," he smiles at me. "Christmas cheer incoming!"

Inside the Yule Love It Boutique, Archer, Gail and I shop every aisle. They're all overloaded with holiday-themed gifts, and I admit I feel my Christmas cheer resurfacing. This is pretty fun.

Gail admires some beautiful things. "I like to get each of my girls an ornament every year, that will always remind them of me."

"What a sweet idea," I tell her.

"Well at this point, my daughter says half her tree is things from me!"

"Nothing like gathering around the tree together," I say, thinking about the many Christmases with my own parents.

"Oh, my girls live in Florida so we can't do that. But this is a way I can reach across the miles. So they always remember me. Even after I'm gone."

That seems to touch a chord in Archer. "Do you think there's Christmas spirit in memories?" he asks Gail.

She stops and pats his hand. "Of course there is, honey. What do you think Christmas spirit is, anyway? It's all about making memories." She leans in closer to him. "The trick is, you have to plan how to make those memories, or the years just fly by with nothing to show for it."

It's a moment of meaning for all three of us, right there in the bustling little gift shop.

Gail grabs a couple of big, sparkly ornaments. "How about these?"

"I love them!" I take them from her and hold one up on either side of her face. "Perfect earrings for you."

Gail laughs. "Those do suit me, darlin'!"

Archer smiles, but he seems lost in far-away thoughts right now.

POPPY CARTER

* * *

As Gail pays for her ornaments, I speak quietly to
Archer. "I feel bad for Gail, not being with her family on
Christmas."

"There are all kinds of family," he says. "I think Gail
might have a wonderful Christmas."

I follow his gaze to see Gail giggling as Willie joins
her at the counter. Gail looks like a girl in love. It makes
me smile.

"Maybe there's hope for all of us," Archer says.

Once more I feel that warmth in my chest, and a heat
on my cheeks. I tell myself he's talking about Gail, not me.

Gail comes back toward us. "Can we do one more
thing, sweetie?"

"Of course!" I'm not ready for this time with Gail to
end. "Where else would you like to shop?"

"I'd like to make a wish at the Christmas Wishing
Tree."

* * *

We make our way back to the big beautiful town tree,
and there are quite a few townspeople around now. Gail
writes her wish, as does Willie. They playfully hide their
wishes from each other as they fold them, and I can't help
thinking they're both hoping for time together.

Celia sidles up to me. "Go ahead, make your wish."

66

I notice Archer is listening to us. I say, "Oh, it's so obvious.

"Obvious?" asks Archer.

I hesitate. "Yes, it's the FAMCO account, of course."

"Emmie! You know the rules. If you say it out loud, it won't come true!"

Celia's mostly joking. Whit laughs, and puts an arm around Celia. It's a moment of Christmas joy. We all watch Gail and Willie flirt by the tree.

"You know what, guys?" says Whit. "This was a really fun, really special night."

"Even without a plan?" says Archer.

Celia chimes in. "It felt kind of special to just let things happen…" But she turns to me and adds, "Of course you know I love a good plan too!"

"That's good, because tomorrow night? Holiday Charades!"

Celia is thrilled. "You mean we can spend another night together?"

"Yep! 7 o'clock at-"

Before I can finish, Archer cuts me off. "At my place."

I'm surprised. Pleasantly. Celia gives me another private "*he liiiiiiikes you*" look, which just makes me shake my head and laugh.

* * *

After all is said and done, Archer and I walk home together. I mean, not together-together, but just because we happen to live in the same direction and we were leaving Tinsel Corners at the same time and…never mind, you get it.

"Okay, I admit it," I tell him. "That was fun tonight."

"It's not a competition you know."

I smile at him, nodding.

He continues, "But if it was a competition, I definitely won the first round."

I have to laugh, and I even give him a little shove in the arm.

"Well get ready for round two! And thanks for having charades at your house. I'll bring everything tomorrow – food too."

"I can handle the food," he says. "It's my turn to muster some magic."

We slow as we come to the place where our paths diverge.

"Okay then," he says. "I guess…"

"See you tomorrow night?"

It's almost like he doesn't want to part. I stand there waiting for him to answer me, and once again "Don't think about kissing Archer" is doing me absolutely no good.

"Goodnight?" I try again.

And this time Archer snaps out of it, nodding and waving goodbye. As we start to turn our separate ways, my phone rings.

"It's Kat," I tell him.

I click on the video call and we can clearly see Kat in her restaurant kitchen. "Emmie? And oh good, Archer too.

Listen you two, I am so sorry, but the party room is not going to be available for your party on Christmas Eve after all. That cancellation was cancelled, if you know what I mean."

Archer and I look at each other. Back to square one.

FIFTEEN

I wake up feeling full of purpose. I make my international calls, and I do every bit of the dirty work that I can, involved with planning this emergency merger whatever-it-is, because I don't want to bother Orion over his break. I get a lot done, but I quickly realize my sense of purpose was about something else too. I also order flowers for the proposal party and explore potential menu ideas.

The village library is having its annual Children's Holiday Story Hour today, and there's even a person in an Elf costume to greet visitors. All the kids are so cute as I walk through, trying not to interrupt.

In his usual back corner, Archer sits staring at his computer screen, motionless. Out of the corner of his eye, he spots me – and breaks into a smile. That makes my heart soar, even though I don't want it to. Archer and I do not live in the same place, like the same things, or have anything in common. The end.

"Is this a bad time?" I ask.

"Yes, but not because of you." He flips his laptop shut. "I could probably use a few minutes of diversion. What's up?"

I flip open my planning notebook. "I called about that hotel ballroom. We'd have to do the party earlier and be out of there by 7:30pm on Christmas Eve, but it could work. Make it a cocktail hour."

"Sure."

"Not ideal," I admit. "But I think we're out of options."

"It will be fine."

We both nod. Unenthusiastic, but resigned to the idea.

"So I guess I'll go finalize it."

"I hate to make you do all the work."

"It's honestly not a problem."

"Okay."

I nod. It's time for me to go. What am I doing standing here like an idiot? "Okay." I turn to leave.

"Wait."

"What is it?" I ask him.

Archer looks around, thinking deeply.

"Did you want to show me your author photo again?" I ask.

"Uh, I don't believe I was the one who brought that out."

71

I have to laugh. "Okay, okay."

"Emmie, what do you think of this?" He motions around him.

"The periodicals corner?"

"The library! We could have Whit and Celia's engagement party here."

I'm not sure it will work, but I immediately get excited. "Tell me more."

"The library's closed for the holidays after today. I could talk to them – I'm kind of a regular here, you know."

"A party inside the library…I kinda love it."

Archer returns my smile. He's truly gratified that I like it, I can tell.

Now my wheels are turning. "The theme could be 'The Christmas Story of Us.'"

"I see what you did there."

"We'd need some lights over here, and here."

"Obviously we'd be augmenting their existing decorations with Christmas cheer overload."

"Obviously!" I laugh, getting really excited. "Let's finalize it!"

"Don't you mean, let's *book* it?"

* * *

As I'm walking home, I'm bursting with the good news. There's one person I really want to discuss this party with and of course it's the one person I can't: Celia. Still, I feel like stopping by the radio station to see how she is.

I'm about to cross the street when I see Celia and Whit together. They step out of the radio station, and it looks like they're in the middle of a heated conversation. I've never seen them talk like that, and I feel like I'm intruding even though they are standing in the middle of Main Street, literally. Celia seems upset, and it takes everything in me not to run to her and try to help. But this is clearly something between the two of them, so I turn and head home without looking back. They deserve their privacy and I am sure it's nothing.

* * *

That night as I walk up to Archer's little cottage, I'm really surprised. He has tasteful Christmas lights and a wreath on the front door. It's understated, but it is decorated. The windows glow with the promise of fun happening inside.

I step on the porch and before I can knock, the door opens. It's Archer, looking handsome. He almost seems younger right now, standing there with his hair still a little damp from the shower, wearing a soft green pullover sweater.

"Hi," he says. But inside of that hi was not just hello, but you look great, and I'm so glad you're here, and I've been waiting for you.

"Hi," I reply. And I hope he can't tell all the things inside of mine. "I like your decorations."

"I put them up just for you."

My heart skitters in my chest, lifted by the possibilities of this man before me. "Um…thanks?" I say. I don't think we've actually broken eye contact yet.

But that all changes when Whit pokes his head out the door. "Great, you're here!" He calls back over his shoulder to Celia, "Emmie's here!"

* * *

We sit next to Archer's perfect little Christmas tree, which I now wonder if he put up just for tonight. A spirited game of Holiday Charades is in progress – me and Archer vs Celia and Whit.

Celia acts out a clue for Whit's benefit and he shouts guesses: "Round… ornament? Falling – snow! Snow ball! Snow – circle? Snow man!... Snow globe!"

"Yes!!"

Whit and Celia celebrate. They are a couple in love.

"You two are a great team," says Archer.

I'm not sure if I'm imagining the little cloud that passes through Celia. But I doubt anyone else even notices.

Celia looks through the clue cards I've made, all of them handwritten and decorated with drawings and glitter. "I love snow globes. And sleigh bells, and the Christmas Wishing Tree. These are great clue cards, Emmie!"

"I made them with you in mind. Personalized holiday charades just for us."

Whit gives me a knowing smile and mouths "thanks."

Archer is looking through the cards now too. "But this game is so good, you could probably market it to anyone."

I'm flattered, but talking about any career other than corporate events just makes me uncomfortable. So I change the subject. "Okay, Mr. Host, you said you'd be in charge of refreshments."

Archer gets a funny look on his face. "Oh yeah. About that…"

Is he just trying to prank me? "You're kidding, right?"

Archer shrugs. "Hey, I've been very busy staring at my computer screen all afternoon, having writer's block."

He and I go to his kitchen and start poking around the cupboards and fridge.

He explains, "I mean, I *remembered*, but then I thought we'd just sort of wing it. See what looks good, what we're hungry for. Look, gingerbread."

"How much?"

"One cookie."

I feel totally frustrated by his lack of effort. "I mean, I get that you like to be all free-and-easy and go-with-the-flow, but with food? Really?"

"Emmie, it's okay. We're not going to starve. Relax."

"Has saying 'relax' to anyone ever actually made them relax?"

Why does this man push my buttons? He makes me so crazy. One moment I'm thinking about how soft that green cashmere sweater would feel if he wrapped his arms around me, and the next I'm thinking that I've never met someone more annoying.

He steps toward me, and gives me a concerned look. "You okay?"

"I'm sorry. Even I wish I could lighten up sometimes." My half laugh is not entirely sincere.

He leans against the counter and speaks to me gently. "Emmie, is it not real unless it's already been put in the notebook? I mean, why do you think you like all the fun to be organized in advance?"

He reaches out and touches my hand, rubbing it softly. I feel myself opening up, responding to his gentle kindness.

"That's a good question. I guess it just makes me feel…secure." I don't want to keep talking, but then again I don't want Archer to stop rubbing my hand. "When I was little, my dad traveled all the time for work, even at Christmas – so my mom would have all this stuff planned for me and her. Crafts, baking, decorating. We had some much fun. The plan just made me feel safe. And happy."

"Sounds like your dad missed a lot. That couldn't have been easy for him."

I never really think about it like that. And I don't want to right now either.

"So what, did you think we'd go hunt and gather for

food?" I point out the window, where big fat snowflakes fall.

Archer looks at the snow, then at me. "Great idea, Emmie."

Not long after, the four of us are around the kitchen island, scooping fluffy snow ice cream into our individual serving dishes.

Whit takes a bite and moans with pleasure. "Snow ice cream is 1000% better than any store-bought ice cream."

Archer takes his one cookie and crushes it. "How about some gingerbread crumbles on that?"

I grab a candy cane off the Christmas tree and hold it up. "And crushed peppermint toppings as well?"

Archer gives me a look that stirs something inside me. He teases, "Emmie, did you just come up with a great snack idea off the cuff?"

"Not off the cuff. Off the tree."

Celia savors her ice cream. "This may be the best dessert ever."

Archer winks at me. "Team effort."

I smile back at Archer and feel a distinct buzzing – but wait, it's not true love, it's my cell phone. "Sorry, the office is calling me."

Celia frowns. "Now? This late in the day?"

"FAMCO is international. I guess it's 8am somewhere." No one laughs at my lame joke.

As I step onto Archer's back porch to take the call, I

think I get a glimpse of disappointment on his face. Or maybe it's irritation. Was it rude of me to take this call? Hey, a girl's gotta make a living.

"Hello?"

"Heeeeey!" It's Orion.

"Oh, I'm so glad it's you. For a second I thought it was Mr. M again."

Orion gives me a wide-eyed look, and reveals that Mr. M is next to him.

"Emmie, I need an update," Mr. M says in his usual no-nonsense way.

"I don't have my notes with me."

"I'm sure you know it all by heart. Go ahead and brief me on the arrangements you've made. FAMCO is nervous. The merger is potentially huge for them. This meeting has to be perfect."

Deep breath, and I start in explaining everything I've arranged so far, as best as I can remember it all.

SIXTEEN

By the time I go back inside after my call, only Celia's in the kitchen. She's straightening up.

"You must be frozen!" she says to me. "The guys are building a fire in the fireplace. How was your call?"

I take a seat at the island as Celia fills a cup with hot tea for me.

"The call was fine. More of the same. Things are looking good for the FAMCO account, assuming no snafus." I idly toy with a snow globe that's on the counter. I shake it and watch the snow fall on North Haven, over and over.

"Well, that's good, right?" says Celia.

I look at my best friend of many years, and know I can tell her anything. "Sometimes I look at my life, and I'm like – how did I become this person in New York who 'does brunch' and rides the subway and speaks fluent spreadsheet?"

"I think it sounds pretty cool."

We both laugh, but it's not very happy laughter. Celia puts her hand over mine. I feel like I'm whining and I hate that.

"I mean, I'm living the dream, right?"

Celia nods. "Sure. But whose dream?"

I stare down at Celia's hand thoughtfully, taking a long beat. "I just realized something."

"What?" asks Celia.

"You need a manicure! The question could be popped at anytime!"

Celia laughs, and shushes me. "Whit will hear you. Anyway, you know what, I'm having such a fun week, I'm not going to look ahead."

"Oh my gosh, you've been hanging around Archer too much!"

* * *

Back in the living room, the guys have built a great fire.

"Okay! Who's up for round two of charades?" I ask.

Archer puts down the fireplace poker. "Charades was great, but I don't know if I have another round in me."

I am so surprised by his demeanor. I'd expected that

same fun we were having earlier, but it seems to be over. Mr. Serious has arrived.

"Of course," I say.

He continues, "I have a big day of writing tomorrow."

"You don't need to explain," I tell him as I gather my things. "We'll get out of your way."

"Well, I didn't mean right this second."

"No, no. I should go too." I'm feeling rattled, and if I'm honest, rejected by Archer.

"Emmie, don't you want to finish your tea?" asks Celia.

"No thanks." I'm already putting on my coat.

I see Whit and Celia exchange a look, and they follow suit. "We should go too."

"Are you sure?" asks Archer. "Emmie?"

"I really do have a lot to do tomorrow too," I tell Archer. "After all, nothing's more important than work." I'm not sure why I say this.

But I can tell it affects Archer. "Right. Me too."

"Right," I answer.

He looks at me, and I hold his gaze. It occurs to me maybe we're both being stubborn here, but too late now.

"Ready?" I say to Whit and Celia.

Celia says, "So should we get together again tomorrow night?"

"Oh sorry, hon," Whit tells her. "I'm working the late shift tomorrow."

Archer picks up one of the glitter-edged cards I made.

"What about the charades clues?"

"We're done with them, just throw them away."

One of them hasn't been unfolded yet. He reaches down and looks at it, then up at me. I try to think what I put on all of them, but I'm not sure.

"Kiss under the mistletoe," he reads.

"Goodnight then," I say. "Happy writing."

"Goodnight, Emmie."

And we walk out the door.

* * *

Whit and Celia drop me off. When we pull up, Celia gets out to give me a hug goodnight. She holds me tightly for a moment longer than usual, as the fat snowflakes float down around us.

Celia whispers to me, "Hey, remember that Christmas you decided at the very last minute to have a sledding party for the whole neighborhood?"

I smile at the memory. "You want to go sledding right now?"

"Emmie, it's not too late to change your life."

"I'm not sure a sledding party is life-changing."

"I'm serious. It's never too late to make a different choice."

"I love you, Celia. But sometimes it really is too late."

She gives me a sad look. But I try to lighten the mood. "What are you gonna do? Adulting! Am I right?"

I wave as they drive away, then head inside. I'm bound and determined to "adult" the heck out of tomorrow. FAMCO merger meeting, look out.

SEVENTEEN

Is it possible my mom has added even more Christmas decorations inside this house overnight? Everywhere I look, it's glitter and ornaments and lights. I sit on the floor, surrounded by our old holiday photo albums. I'm picking out pictures we have of Celia from Christmases throughout the years. I think I might be able to use them at the surprise party.

My dad sits in his favorite chair nearby, one of the only things in the room not festooned with tinsel, and reads the newspaper.

"Hey Em, I DVR'ed *Undercover Executive* – have you seen the new episode?"

"Um, no." I am busy looking at 11-year-old me wearing a sequined Santa hat. Not my best year, with pre-braces teeth and that shag haircut I begged to get.

"The Undercover Executive takes over a failing

bakery and turns it into a mortgage and title business!"

Dad's bright enthusiasm is hard to match. I give him a distracted smile. "Sounds great, Dad."

He looks over the top of his newspaper. "What are you working on there?"

"Hopefully this is going to be a wall of photos at the engagement party. 'The Christmas Story of Us' – with the whole history of Whit and Celia's growing up and falling in love."

"Cute." He goes back to his newspaper.

"Dad?"

"Mm hmm?" He turns the page of his newspaper.

"Did you have to work holidays a lot when I was little?"

"I guess."

"Even at Christmas?"

He lowers the newspaper, and squints at me. "Sure, especially in the early years."

"You must've missed a lot of fun with me and Mom. Making reindeer chow and delivering it to the neighbors. Wrapping gifts at the community center."

"Oh yes, Mom always had so many activities planned for you."

"…Were you ever sad to miss out?"

Dad considers that for a moment. "It's never easy. But knowing I was providing a secure life for you and Mom made it all worthwhile." He gives me a warm, happy smile. But then tilts his head, as if curious what I'm thinking.

The doorbell rings. Amazon strikes again. Packages that my mom ordered have been arriving constantly.

I jump to see what this latest is. I'm still not above shaking a box to try and guess what's inside. I open the door.

"Archer!" He stands on my front porch, looking a tiny bit nervous. "What are you doing here?"

"Oh hey," he says, as if he's surprised to run into me here. At my house. On my front porch. After he rang the doorbell.

"I had a productive morning of writing. And then I remembered you had set aside this time to work on the photo wall, so-"

"That's the plan."

He reacts to that word, but I don't smile back. "I come bearing photographs. From Whit's family archives."

"You what?"

Sure enough, I glance to see some gloriously awkward childhood photos of Whit. I can't hide my grin. "Come on in."

Dad must've assumed it was a deliveryman as well, because when he sees me leading a tall, dark, handsome guy into our living room, he's clearly surprised. He puts aside the paper and stands up.

"Hello there."

"Dad, this is Archer Mendez."

They shake, and Archer mumbles, "Nice to meet you, sir."

"Aw, the local celebrity! Nice to meet you too. Janelle loved your book – what was it? Christmas – ?"

"*Holiday Magic*," I say.

"That's the one! Emmie's mom loves those happily ever afters."

Archer stands up straight and looks a tiny bit nervous. What's going on with him? "Thank you, Mr. Andrews."

Awkward much? This room feels so uncomfortable all the sudden.

I say, "Archer brought some photos" at the same moment Dad says, "Well, I'll leave you two" and then Archer overlaps with "Your house is beautiful."

More silence descends, as apparently the three of us have forgotten how to have a conversation.

"Em, I'll leave you two," Dad tries again.

"That's okay, we're just organizing the party."

Dad winks at me, and I remember the cold sweat of middle school embarrassment.

"Oh, I might have to finish up some Christmas shopping," he says.

Dad leaves, and Archer pretends to be fascinated with our Christmas tree.

"Can I get you anything? Cocoa?"

"I'm more of a hot chocolate person." He gives me a look but I'm not ready to match his energy. "Just kidding, I don't need anything."

I start sifting through the photos Archer brought, and they are solid gold. The photo wall is going to be so funny.

For instance, there are photos of both Celia and Whit in Power Ranger Halloween costumes – separately of course, decades before they even met. Talk about meant for each other.

"Is this you?" Archer says. He's found a framed photo ornament on the tree and brings it over.

It's young me showing off a pair of spangled holiday socks.

"No comment."

"What are you wearing here? The things we used to do, am I right?"

He's attempting humor, but I just sigh.

He might as well know. I raise my pant leg to show: I'm wearing glittery, spangly, silly Christmas socks right now. Archer's reaction says, whoa.

"I have quite an extensive collection. Some might call it an obsession. Ugly Christmas sweaters are so…overt. But these? I've been making them since I was little."

Archer has to laugh. "I love them. Normal to the outside world, but secretly a Christmas party fanatic."

I shrug. "It's funny 'cause it's true."

I go ahead and get both of us some hot cocoa, and pretty soon we are settled in at the dining room table, surrounded by old photos.

"This one's great," says Archer.

"Oh yeah, definitely!"

"So many amazing Christmas memories here."

"What's your best Christmas memory, Archer?" I

wonder if I'm being too forward, considering his past, but then again it's an innocent question.

"Hmm. If you'd asked me that last week, I probably would have said it was the year I got a razor scooter, sprained my wrist immediately, so my parents let me eat all the candy Santa put in my stocking in one day."

"That's hard to beat."

"But now I might say that I'm not sure if I've had my best one yet."

There's a beat of connection that I think we're both feeling. And both denying.

Archer clears his throat. "So any word on that big account in New York?"

"Not yet. But I'm feeling really hopeful."

"That's great."

Something in the way he says 'great' just rubs me the wrong way.

"It's an incredible job, you know," I say, trying to keep the defensiveness in my voice to a minimum. "A lot of people would love to organize corporate conferences for FAMCO."

He smiles and nods. "Of course." Then he nods and smiles again.

"And it's important work. These things really affect their bottom line. And team morale. You'd be surprised."

"I don't think anyone's arguing with you, Emmie."

I take a deep breath. "Sorry."

"Unless you're arguing with yourself? Because you

kind of secretly like some other kind of planning?"

Something about the way he sees me so clearly makes me open up a little. I don't want to – but the old photos and the cocoa and the twinkling lights of the tree and, okay, I admit it – the way Archer looks at me, have created this intimacy that I'm not used to.

"When I was about twelve, my dad got laid off," I say. "It was a sketchy time for us – no money coming in. My parents were always whispering, they didn't think I knew."

"That must've been scary for a kid."

"Yeah. It was then that I realized how important it is to have a steady job to count on."

"I get that. But it's important to follow your dreams too."

"Maybe my dream is to be secure," I say, wondering if in fact that's true.

Archer checks the time. "Oh! We have to go."

I'm confused. "What do you mean?"

"I made a plan for tonight."

"But –"

"Surprised?"

"Let's just say I'll believe it when I see it."

Archer laughs. "Come on, Celia's expecting us."

EIGHTEEN

We pick up Celia, and drive downtown to park. Archer leads the two of down Main Street. He's being quite mysterious and clearly enjoying that we don't know what's happening.

"Okay, seriously. Where are we going?" I ask.

Archer stops in front of the fire station. "Here. I thought we'd see if the firefighters could use some Christmas fun."

Crickets, as we wait for further details. But none are forthcoming, just Archer looking at us with an expectant smile.

Celia elbows me. "What a great idea!"

I want to be the fun, relaxed holiday girl – but what is he talking about. "Yeah, okay. How will we do that?"

"That's where the winging-it part comes in." And Archer heads inside, a bounce in his step.

I roll my eyes, but Celia laughs. She links arms with me and pulls us forward.

Inside this happy hometown fire station is an actual dalmatian (so adorable) and half a dozen firefighters sitting around watching a Christmas movie.

Whit's happily surprised to see us.

"What are you all doing here?"

Archer answers, "Just wondering if the firehouse could use a little Christmas cheer overload? As in, a holiday party?"

Whit looks around to his co-workers. "Yeah, sure, I guess."

The other firefighters nod in agreement.

"Great!" Archer's enthused.

And then we all stand around looking at each other. I find these moments beyond awkward. Try excruciating. Try nails-on-a-chalkboard downright painful as everyone stands around wondering what's next…

Finally, I can't stand it. "Do you all have a speaker I can sync up with? Let's at least play some holiday tunes."

Archer's smile gets even bigger.

And so I connect my phone to their speaker, and Christmas music takes over the room. Celia and I poke around the fire house kitchen, creating impromptu Reindeer Cookies out of pretzels and some candies they have on hand. Archer has brought the Christmas charades cards I made, and I have to admit as he pulls them out, I feel a little touched that he didn't trash them. A raucous game of Christmas charades ensues, round after round of hilarity. Archer and I wind up making some snow ice cream too. The truth is, it's a great party. One of the best I've ever attended, much less planned.

Archer and I stand to the side, observing everyone having a great time.

"This is so fun," I admit.

"It's almost like we're a good team," he says.

"Almost."

This time when we share a smile of connections, it's like we're going to give over to it. I mean, why not? Yes, we're different. Yes, we live in separate places. Yes, we just met. Yes yes yes, there are a million no's. But in this moment, Archer's genuine smile and the twinkle in his eyes have me all like I-think-I'm-falling-in-like…

And my phone dings. Because of course. I glance at it and shove it back in my pocket.

"Everything okay?" Archer asks, oh-so-casually.

"Just a lot of prep still up in the air for this merger meeting. I worked on it all day before you came over, but there are still loose ends."

"Who has a corporate meeting on Christmas Eve?"

"That's what I said. Executives who want to arrange a merger out of the public eye. It's the board of directors from two huge companies, all getting together in total privacy. They swoop in for a few hours in their private jets, have this buy-out vs merger discussion, all shrouded in secrecy."

"Sounds pretty important."

"Hundreds of jobs hang in the balance." My phone dings again. It's Orion. "So sorry, I should take this."

"Of course."

Somehow the fun goes out of the party by the time I'm through with my work call. I help clean up a bit, and then Whit and Celia give me a ride home.

* * *

Mom has waited up for me. I give her a hug.

"Hey sweetie. Dad already went to bed." She pours me a cup of hot tea. "Did you have fun tonight?"

"Yeah, it was really great." I can tell that doesn't sound entirely sincere. "Except work called. It's a little annoying. I mean I'm grateful for the job of course-"

"Of course." She gives my arm a squeeze. "How was Archer?"

"Good. I don't know. Confusing. One minute friendly, then he goes cold." I sip my tea. It's the perfect temperature and warms me to my core.

"Sometimes when people have been hurt, they're reluctant to open up."

"I know you're right. I am not sure what I'm expecting. It doesn't matter anyway. He lives here, not in New York."

"People move sometimes." Mom smiles.

"True. But there's something else too."

"What's that?"

"We're completely incompatible."

She laughs. "Oh, that little thing."

"I love you, Mom. Thanks for the tea."

I head upstairs, suddenly ready to sink into my canopy bed and dream away my worries…

As if that ever happens.

NINETEEN

The next morning as soon as I get my FAMCO emails and phone calls done, I head back to the library. This time it has a *Closed for the Holidays* sign, but the door is unlocked and I go on inside. Archer's waiting for me, lost in thought.

"Hi," I say.

He jumps a little. "Oh, I didn't hear you come in."

"What were you thinking about?"

"Oh, just my book. Which is actually not a book yet, since it doesn't have an ending."

"Wanna talk about it?"

"Absolutely not!" He laughs, but there's not a lot of humor behind it.

I change the subject. "What if we brought in an arbor?"

"A what?"

I flip through my notebook, and show him. "You

know, some posts holding up an arch. We'd cover it in Christmas greenery and twinkle lights. So romantic. And spell out 'Will you marry me?' across it."

"Over the top?"

"Yes, right over the top of their heads."

"No, I mean isn't that over the top. They're not getting married. At least not yet."

I want to be collaborative – well "want" is a strong word. I am trying to be collaborative.

"I guess you're right," I say. "Arbors are romantic, but it might be too much." I mark it off my list. "We definitely need a really big Christmas tree though."

"It might be hard to get one, this close to Christmas. The tree lot by my house is practically empty."

Hmm. "What if we built the tree out of books? Stack them up, in a sort of round pyramid?"

"A round pyramid. And how was geometry for you, Emmie?"

"You know what I mean!" He makes me smile. "We could build a tree out of books."

"So people could check it out? Get it – like a library book?"

"If a joke falls flat in the forest, does anybody laugh?"

"Is that your way of telling me we have to make a whole forest of library book Christmas trees?"

My phone rings and I literally groan. I am getting so sick of work calls. But turns out it's Celia. Archer excuses himself to unload some decorations we both have out in our cars, and I answer Celia's call.

She sounds upset, immediately launching into a rather confusing narrative about how Kat, the restaurant owner, has said she was sorry about Christmas Eve. Celia has created a whole conspiracy theory about how Whit had been planning to propose to her but has gotten cold feet and now backed out.

"Emmie, I am pretty sure Whit never wants to get married. He acts so weird if I even get close to the subject, like really secretive and honestly just sketchy. I mean, I just wish he'd be honest with me instead of avoiding the subject." There's a catch in Celia's voice, as if she's holding back tears.

It's hard to know what to say, because I don't want to betray Whit's secret but I also cannot stand to see my friend hurting like this. I blather on about how much Whit loves her, but I can tell she thinks I don't understand what's happening. She gets called away at work and has to hang up quickly, so we are cut short. I sit and wonder what's best, but I know in just a couple of days this will all be worked out. When she walks into this surprise party, all will be forgiven.

* * *

Archer and I make some great progress, stringing lights and putting up decorations. The open space in the central part of the library is a beautiful room anyway, and now it's turning into a romantic Christmas wonderland. I sense that party inspo energy churning inside of me, and it's a great feeling.

"Let's do all red ornaments here, in the shape of a heart."

"Anyone ever told you that you have a gift for this stuff?" says Archer.

I shrug. "Nah, I just like it."

"Can't you see that *is* your gift?"

He turns out the overhead fluorescents, and we are lit just by the Christmas lights. It looks downright dreamy. Who knew a library could be so romantic.

"See what you've done, Emmie? The love of doing something is what makes you good at it."

"I never thought of it exactly like that. Thanks, Archer. And I guess that's why you're a writer."

He lets out an abrupt laugh. "Hmm, maybe you just disproved my writing because right now, I am not enjoying writing at all."

"But that's just a temporary writer's block. You used to love it, didn't you?"

"I've always made up stories, since I was little. And it used to come easy. When I wrote *Holiday Magic*, it seemed simple, straightforward. People could live happily ever after. Presto."

I let the moment of silence just exist for a moment.

I turn toward him. "I'm sorry about how you lost your fiancée. Celia told me about it."

"Oh, you two were talking about me?" It's a weak attempt at humor, and neither of us smile.

"She just told me that your fiancée got sick unexpectedly, before you even got married."

"It was several years ago. My book had just come out, everything looked rosy. But then when it happened...I realized you can't count on the future."

I reach out and put a hand on his arm. I can feel his pain, and I've never seen him quite so vulnerable.

He puts his hand over mine. "You have to live in the moment. You can't spend all your time planning for something that might never happen, Emmie."

"I can see how you might have felt that way. But there are always things to look forward to."

We're standing quite close now, surrounded by the sparkling glow of string lights, all alone.

"No, I don't believe there always is something good in the future. At least, that's how I'm wired now."

"So there's nothing to look forward to?"

He reaches up and touches my cheek, and the electricity fills me head to toe.

"I do like you, Emmie."

I can't believe I'm saying this, but: "I like you too."

Are we going to kiss? Somehow our bodies have gotten closer and closer. I can feel the heat of his chest near mine.

"Emmie, being around you is the first time in a long time that I've felt –" He doesn't finish that thought. "But obviously we approach life very differently."

"Maybe that's a good thing?" I counter. "Balance each other out. Together, we've gotten quite a bit done this week."

"That's all due to your plans."

"Last night, at the fire station, how everything came together in the moment. That felt pretty special."

Our faces are so close now. I let down my defenses. If this is wrong, sign me up.

Archer doesn't move, but I see him staring at my mouth. I have to go up on my tiptoes for my mouth to reach his – the barest, briefest little touch of our lips sends a shudder through my entire being. I did not know barely kissing could be like this. Now he reaches forward, brushing his lips against mine again, quickly and softly.

BUZZZ….

"Is that your phone?" His voice is a whisper, and not a happy one.

"I should really start turning this thing off," I joke.

BUZZZ…. We don't move a muscle.

"But you don't really want to do that, do you?" Archer takes a step back. "Because your job's important to you. Go ahead and answer your call. I have to go write anyway. We can finish up all of this tomorrow."

I'm shocked, confused. What just happened? Is this love or hate or worst of all, just indifference? Archer stares at me, dispassionately. I reach in my pocket and pull out the dreaded phone.

"Hello, this is Emmie."

Archer exhales and turns away, starts packing up his stuff.

I put the phone on speaker, it's Orion. "Oh my gosh, Emmie. Crisis mode activated. Apparently we also need a live-feed video call on the big screen, with their Taipei office now. I don't know how to do that. Mr. M is having a menty-b right now."

I keep my eyes on Archer, who gives me a friendly wave goodbye as he heads for the door.

"Okay, Orion, no worries. Tell me what's happening and I'll walk you through it." I don't have any scratch paper with me, so I open up my party notebook and turn it to a clean page.

TWENTY

When I get home, Mom and Dad are watching a Christmas movie, but I rush past them.

"What's up, sweetie?" says Mom.

"Nothing. I have to go do some work stuff on my computer real quick."

"Why, what happened?"

"Oh, they want to connect the Taipei office. Which creates a few security issues with the venue, who do not have protected wifi. But all good. I can handle it from here."

Dad's antenna go up. "What do you mean? Did they want you to go into the office? Shouldn't you go back to New York?"

"Dad, I'm hosting a surprise party in two days, on Christmas Eve."

"It's the engagement, Phil. You know that."

He shakes his head. "Sometimes you have to put off fun when work calls."

"I mean, I can't exactly put it off. This is a one-time thing. This party is a really important night for Celia's whole future."

"And this corporate merger could be a really important thing for your future, Emmie."

When parents are right, it's so annoying.

At that moment, another text from Orion arrives: *S.O.S. I accidentally deleted the agenda memo!*

Sigh. "Dad, let's talk about this later. I have to go call work."

And I rush upstairs.

Back in my office-slash-canopy-bed, I finish up all the arrangements for the Taipei video feed to be fully secure. I rip that page out of my notebook, not wanting to have it mixed in with my childhood dreams.

* * *

The next morning, I'm on my way to Cake My Day to finalize their catering for the party. As I walk to the bakery, I'm finishing up yet another phone call with my assistant.

"Orion, you've got this! You are not going to be fired, please stop worrying." We sign off, fingers crossed for everything to go well at the FAMCO merger meeting.

I head up toward the bakery counter, waiting my turn, when I notice a woman in front of me huffing impatiently.

She must be in her 70s, dressed head to toe in black business attire. I wonder idly who she is and what she's doing here, when I hear:

"I am looking for Mr. Archer Mendez, I heard he comes here?"

The young barista is hesitant to offer private information.

"Helloooo? Blink if you can hear me," says the woman in black.

"Hi, I'm Emmie Andrews. May I help you?"

The woman spins away from the young barista toward me, narrowing her eyes. She obviously does not suffer fools gladly.

"I'm looking for Archer Mendez, the renowned novelist. He apparently frequents this establishment occasionally. Have you ever seen him here?"

"Um yes, I know Archer."

"I'm Maude Miller, his literary agent. How do you do?"

Maude has a firm, confident handshake. Beyond firm – almost painful.

"Nice to meet you, Maude."

Once Maude and I are situated at a table with our coffees, she starts questioning me.

"So does Archer come to this place often?"

"Yes, as the matter of fact, I'm meeting him here today."

"You're not that radio announcer, are you? He never should've done an interview without checking with me first."

"No, that's not me."

"Are you the librarian that lets him stay there all day?"

"Not me either."

"Then who are you?"

"Well, there's an existential question." Maude doesn't smile so I continue. "I'm just a friend. We're arranging a party together-"

"Ah, the party planner."

I admit I'm thrilled to know Archer mentioned me. Then again, it sounds like he's mentioned everyone he knows in North Haven. "Yes ma'am, I guess that's me."

Her eyes narrow. "He didn't mention you were pretty."

"Well…thank you?"

"Interesting." She looks me up and down in a disconcerting way. "I'm sorry, dear. But I have to protect Archer. He's quite sensitive, and he's been through a lot. When things upset him, he can't write. We can't have that happen, can we?"

"I would not want Archer to be upset, no."

"Good girl." She gives me a nod. "And I wanted to thank you."

Now I'm really confused. "Thank me for - ?"

"For letting Archer do his research with you."

"Ah. His research." This woman has me rattled. What

research? Should I just say you're welcome and leave?

"Archer had no idea how to write about throwing a party. He's been working on this final chapter of his book for weeks. Months!"

"I did hear him say something about writer's block."

"It was more like writer's wall. He kept saying, how am I ever going to write this final scene. Then this friend of his, William I think?"

"Whit?"

"Whit! Whit had the idea that he knew someone who could show Archer the tricks of the party trade. That must have been you."

I pull my lips into the smile shape, but inside my brain is short-circuiting. I am not loving this story. Does she mean what I think she means?

Maude sips her coffee. "You're a saint to let him do all of this tagging along so he could see what all you do. Those details are really going to add authenticity to the book."

My heart's pounding in a fight-or-flight way. Who is Archer and has all of this just been a ruse so he could finish his book? That's not possible. I think of Archer's smile, of the way I feel when we talk, of the way he makes fun of me. All of that was real, yes?

Yet here's a woman I've never met who seems to know all about me.

And didn't Archer tell me he has nothing to look

forward to? Did he mean that *we* have nothing to look forward to?

My phone dings and I consider throwing it on the ground and stomping on it. Instead I say, "I'm sorry. It's work."

Maude smiles at me, for the first time. "Are you kidding? It's wonderful to be around someone getting a work message. You must have an actual life! Please, go ahead, do your thing. I'm going to get a refill."

As Maude heads to the counter, I read the latest text from Orion: *FAMCO says they will cancel unless you are here in person!!!*

I stare at the phone screen as I listen to Maude explain to the young barista exactly how to foam the oat milk at an angle. I sit there wondering what I should do next, and also passively learning how to make an oat milk latte.

Through the bakery window, I see Archer approaching. He enters and comes right toward me. He doesn't even notice Maude, who by now has moved behind the counter to fulfill her own order.

"Hey, Em. Am I late?"

"Only my friends call me Em."

I can see he is taken aback. "Sorry about that."

I don't say 'that's okay.' I don't ask him to sit down.

"So, are you ready to head to the library?" he asks.

I shake my head.

He slides into the seat next to me, smiling. "Alrighty

then. Is there some sort of party planning crisis I need to know about?"

I don't smile, I don't even react. He begins to realize I'm not joking.

"Listen, Emmie, if this is about last night. I hope you're not mad? Because the last thing I want to do is upset you. And actually, I wanted to talk to you. I need to tell you something."

"How much further do you have to go on your book?"

He wasn't expecting that question. "How much further? Well, it's due tomorrow."

"Have you written the final party scene?"

I can see the wheels turning in his head, as he wonders how I know about that scene, if he somehow mentioned it to me. "Did Whit tell you about that? So, no. I haven't written the party scene. And I don't think it's going to be what the publisher is expecting either." He shrugs, looking unenthused about the novel's ending. "But at least I'll be done."

"So you'll be all finished with your research then?"

I sense a bit of discomfort in Archer's eyes.

"I'm not sure what you're asking me," he says.

Remember that fight or flight feeling? All of the sudden fight rises up. "Were you just helping with the party to research some scene for your book?!"

"No! I mean…not exactly."

"Not *exactly*?" I stare as he fidgets. "That's your answer? Not exactly?"

Archer doesn't respond, just gazes downward. I think I might cry, so I gather my things and rush outside.

I'm in a huge hurry to get out of that bakery, but once I'm on the street, I'm not even sure which direction to walk. I realize Archer is right behind me.

"Emmie, please. What's going on?"

I wheel back toward him. "You know, for some of us, this surprise proposal party is actually a really important, really big life moment. It's not just a fact-finding mission to use in a story."

"Look, I know that. I want them to have a nice party."

"A nice party? We've been planning so much more than a party. Don't you realize that? This was never just about catering details and flower arrangements."

"Emmie, come on-"

"Don't you get it? I thought we were planning –" My voice breaks. "A happily ever after."

Archer holds my gaze for long beat. I'm sure he can see the tears in my eyes. He reaches toward my face, then pulls his hand back before he touches me.

"I'm sorry," he says. "But I just don't believe in fairy tales anymore."

We stand toe to toe, eye to eye.

But not heart to heart.

"Archer Mendez, National Book Award Finalist, there you are!"

He turns around, truly surprised to see his agent. But

now he gets what has happened.

"Maude, what are you doing here?"

"I'm here for my bestselling author. Whatever he needs!"

A few locals walking by the bakery glance over at this loud woman who is bragging about Archer.

"Maude, cool it. Emmie, this is-"

"Oh, we met," says Maude. "Archer, I came to make sure you turn in your manuscript tomorrow." Maude smiles sweetly, but also: don't mess with her. "You sounded a little iffy on the phone yesterday. But I'm here for you."

Archer rubs his hands over his face. "Why don't you come by my house later? Emmie and I have to get to the library and finalize everything for tomorrow."

I finally pipe up, attempting to be cool as a cucumber. "I'm sorry, I can't go the library today."

Archer's the one who's flustered now. "Well, can you go tomorrow morning?"

"I can't go to the library at all." I decide as I speak, "Because I have to go back to New York. For my job. Which is very important to me."

Maude gives me a wink and a smile. "Love that girl boss energy. You go, Emily."

"It's Emmie. But thanks."

Archer looks back and forth between me and Maude. "What about the proposal party?"

"You'll have to finish it. Alone."

"But it won't be the same."

I feel really conflicted about leaving. But every sign in the universe seems to be telling me that my job needs me, and Archer was just using me. "All the plans have basically been made. You can finalize any details on your own."

He thinks on that. "So just order a couple pizzas and we're good?"

I'm not about to smile at any joke Archer Mendez makes.

Maude slips an arm through Archer's. "Well, thanks for everything, Emily."

Archer half-whispers, "It's Emmie."

But Maude doesn't hear him. She continues, "So I guess this is goodbye."

"Goodbye," I say. "And good luck with your research."

I turn and practically jog toward my car. I feel those tears pressing down again, and I'm determined not to cry until I'm in bed with a canopy over my head.

Archer runs after me. "Emmie, your notebook!"

I turn back to see him holding the Emmie's Parties, the notebook that I've had for twenty years. My childish handwriting and the glitter hearts just embarrass me now.

"I don't need it anymore," I say as I get in my car.

TWENTY-ONE

I sit at the kitchen counter, dressed for travel all in black. Not that different than what Maude was wearing, to be honest. It feels usual and routine to be back in business attire, and I don't have to be embarrassed that my phone is dinging and I have my thumbs flying through the messages on it, even as my parents talk to me.

"I packed some cookies for you to take to the office," says Mom.

"We need to get to the train station ten minutes ago," says Dad.

"Tomorrow is Christmas Eve. Am I the only one who thinks it's nuts to be leaving home to go back to the office?" Mom frets.

"You heard what Em said. The whole deal is at risk if things go wrong."

"I just think family holidays are important too, call me crazy."

Dad's voice is edged with impatience. "Maybe the investors in Taipei don't care about which day we open our gifts."

Mom and Dad turn to hear my input. I look back and forth between them, knowing they both want the best for me. What should I say?

"Dad's right. Sometimes you have to choose responsibility in the long term."

Mom sags a tiny bit, then plasters on her loving smile. "I love you," she says.

Dad puffs up a bit. "That's right, Emmie. Sometimes you have to put off moments of togetherness, in favor of a secure future."

Somehow, that doesn't sound like a speech from the final scene of *It's a Wonderful Life*, but I roll with it.

* * *

The next eighteen hours are a blur of calls and emails and requests and emergencies and last-minute changes and texts and contracts and cancellations and demands and re-bookings. And oh yeah, a little bit of sleep. I'm grateful that I don't have time to think about North Haven or Celia and Whit or…any of it. Work is back at the forefront of my mind, like it has been for years.

I lean on Orion's desk while he sits at his computer,

fingers flying. I check things off our list.

"All we have left is to set up the auxiliary room, which is optional. I don't even know if they'll use it. And then the actual video conference hook up, and the meeting begins tonight."

Orion leans back in his chair. "I'm so glad you came back! Thank you. I didn't want to say that I needed you – but I needed you." He laughs.

"Orion, you know what? I'm not sure about that. You actually had everything already done. You kept saying there was trouble, but look at this." I hold up the list. "You arranged all of this."

Orion shrugs, pleased. "I guess I was nervous."

"That's understandable, but you shouldn't have been. To tell you the truth, I thought things were going to be a mess when I arrived!" We share a laugh. "But you had it all under control. Orion, I want you to start believing in yourself. Believe in your dreams."

Orion smiles at me. "I will when you will."

This gives me pause. "I guess I really am my mentor. You're following my footsteps." We have to chuckle.

My phone rings, a video call with Celia. I take it in the outer office. "Hey, what's up?"

Celia's crying. "I'm going to break up with Whit."

"WHAT. Celia, I promise you, Whit loves you."

"But he doesn't want to commit. And life is flying by, Em. I can't keep waiting and waiting. I'm pretty sure he doesn't want to ever get married."

"You don't know that."

Celia is bursting with emotion. "I know that every time anyone even mentions marriage, he gets super nervous. I told him I want someone who can communicate with me!"

Just then, Mr. M walks out to see me. "Emmie, I have a few questions for you."

I hold up my pointy finger in the international symbol for wait-a-second, but Mr. M doesn't seem to know what it means. He just stands there staring at me.

I speak quietly into the phone. "Celia, you and Whit are great together."

"I don't want to force someone to commit."

Mr. M speaks loudly, "Emmie? Did you update those sales figures in the agenda?"

Celia hears him and tries to wipe away her tears. "I'll let you go to work."

"No!" I say to Celia, but she hangs up.

"No you didn't update the sales figures?" says Mr. M.

"They're all done," I tell him.

TWENTY-TWO

I grab a moment alone in my office, and call Celia for the tenth time, but she's not responding to my calls or texts. I'm sure she set her phone aside, and I don't know what to do. I can't let her break up with Whit. Even though it's a misunderstanding, sometimes things can be said that aren't forgiven. I don't want Celia to say something to Whit that she can't take back later. I know they love each other. Maybe I should have told her about the proposal party that was being planned, but I knew Whit dreamt of it being a surprise.

I take a deep breath and do what I thought I'd never do. I call Archer.

It's his voice mail: "Knock-knock, who's there? Not me, so leave a message."

BEEP. "Archer! Listen to me, this is important. It's

Emmie. But that's not the important part. You have to find Whit and make sure he does not see Celia all day. It's important. Like super important!"

Mr. M walks in without knocking, but I continue leaving a message.

"Okay, I know it sounds crazy. But please, just keep those two apart until the party tonight. Bye."

Mr. M is in a celebratory mood. "I think it's going well. Once we get the Taipei feed connected tonight without a hitch, we'll be set. You really are a master of corporate events."

Those are the nicest words I've ever heard come out of this man's mouth.

"I actually didn't do everything on this – a lot of it was Orion."

"Well, he's your employee. Learn to take a compliment, Emmie."

"Sir, respectfully, I have to go now. I have something I have to take care of. I think things are in good hands with Orion."

"Why don't you just wait until the meeting's over? Just a few more hours, and then you can go."

"I'm sorry, that's not going to be possible."

A long beat. I think he's wondering if he can lock the doors and keep me here until the merger goes through.

"Okay, just be back in time for Taipei."

WHAT HAPPENED TO EVERYTHING

When I get off the train in North Haven, the first thing I see is my parents in their car. You know it's a small town when you don't tell anyone you're coming but you run into your own family within two minutes.

"Emmie! You're back already?" says Dad.

"Did your co-workers like the cookies?"

I hug them both hello. "Dad, I left everything in Orion's capable hands for a few hours. And Mom, I hate to say it, but I don't think anyone has had time to have a cookie yet."

Dad's concerned. "Are you sure that Orion can handle it?"

"What I'm sure of, is that I have to go see my best friend Celia right now, and that's the most important thing to me in this moment. And I don't have much time."

Mom smiles at me, but Dad doesn't.

"Can you drop me at the radio station?"

"Fine." Dad's whole vibe right now is kids-these-days, but all I care about is getting to Celia.

What passes for a traffic jam in North Haven is currently occurring on Main Street, which means a teenager trying to parallel park is doing such a poor job they have stopped cars from both directions. So I jump out and run the last block. Just as I'm almost to the radio station, I see Archer and Whit.

"Emmie!" calls Whit. "You're back?"

I purposefully don't look at Archer, but I can feel his discomfort anyway.

119

"Hey Whit."

"Celia is going to be so excited! She didn't think you'd be back for Christmas Eve, with work and all. Let's go see her, all of us."

"NO," Archer and I say in unison.

Whit looks confused. "Okay."

But it doesn't matter, because Celia has seen all of us out her window, and she now comes outside. I'm sure glad I came back to North Haven to fix things, because clearly it's not going exactly like I'd planned.

Celia looks like she's been crying. "What are you doing here?"

I try to think of an answer. "I just came back, I finished, well I didn't finish-"

"I'm not talking to you. I'm talking to Whit," Celia says. "I wanted to talk to you but Archer said you two were going to be busy all day!"

Whit is thoroughly confused. "Archer said we were busy?"

Celia is not having it. "Oh, don't act all innocent with me. You're obviously ignoring me. Avoiding me. Don't worry, you don't have to do that anymore."

Archer says, "Celia, how was your radio show today? Who did you interview? I like your coat, is that new?"

I have to roll my eyes at his total ineptitude.

Celia is not deterred. "Whit, what is going on with you?!"

"Celia, I don't know what you're talking about and I don't like your tone. Do you not trust me?"

Archer tries to hustle Whit away, "Okay pal, we should go."

And I do the same with Celia, "Let's go back inside, sweetie."

Whit says, "Maybe you should have a little faith in me."

Celia's vote rises, tremulous. "I'm sorry, Whit. But I – I don't think we should date anymore."

Whit is beyond shocked. His knees buckle a bit and Archer steadies him.

"Whaaa…."

Archer jumps in, more serious now. "Look, this is a huge misunderstanding. Right, Whit? Just tell Celia what's happening."

But now Whit feels disrespected. "If she doesn't have a faith in me, I have nothing to tell her."

"Oh come on now," I say. "Celia has faith in you!"

Celia is cold as ice. "Do I?"

Whit stares back at her. "I don't really want to spend my life with someone who thinks I'm tricking her or avoiding her. If you can't trust me…" He lets the sentiment float in the air.

Celia and Whit stare at each other.

I put my arm around Celia. "This is truly a mix-up. It's not what you think."

"Or is it?" says Whit.

And both Whit and Celia take off in opposite directions.

I look at Archer. "What. Just. Happened?"

"I think they broke up."

We stare at each other for a beat.

"So…I'll get her there tonight, and you get him there," I say.

"But how?"

"I have no idea."

"Sounds like a plan."

We both nod, then take off in different directions after our best friends.

TWENTY-THREE

I sit at the kitchen island, watching my mom make the key lime pie for tomorrow. It may not be traditional, but it's Dad's favorite and so she makes it every year.

"Have you tried Celia's house?" she asks me.

"Of course. The radio station too – that's where she left her phone. Celia is totally missing and doesn't even have her phone. And it's just four hours until the party."

"What about Whit?"

"Archer texted he'd have him there. But what does that matter if I can't find Celia? Where could she be?" I feel despair creeping up.

"Oh, sweetie. She's so lucky to have a friend like you. All the years you've spent together."

"All the Christmases we've spent together." All the sudden my wheels are turning. "Wait, that reminds me of something-"

But just then, guess what. Of course. Mr. M. I answer just as Dad walks into the kitchen. He does not even attempt to hide the fact he's listening to my call.

"Mr. M! Merry Christmas Eve, again. All okay there?"

"I mean, so far. What time will you be back?"

"As I said, I believe that Orion is more than capable of-"

"I didn't ask you if Orion was capable. I asked what time your train gets back here. The Taipei tele-conference means all hands on deck."

Mom can't hold her tongue any longer. "Working at nine o'clock on Christmas Eve night." She tsk-tsks.

Mr. M may not be able to see her, but he heard her. "That's nine a.m. in Taipei, and Christmas is not a big holiday there."

Dad shushes Mom a bit angrily. I feel the exasperation over everything in my life bubbling over. What Dad wants, what Mom wants, what Mr. M wants, what Archer wants…

What do I want?

"Mr. M," I say, careful to keep my voice measured. "I really enjoy planning these corporate events, and I do understand the necessity of working odd hours, and even some holidays – but right now, I have a personal situation with my best friend. I have to be there for her."

Mr. M is not happy. But what's new? "What are you saying, Ms. Andrews?"

I take a deep breath. What am I saying…? "I'm saying

this position is no longer a good fit for me. Please consider this my two weeks' notice."

My parents both react with total shock. Mom: happy shock, Dad: unhappy shock.

"Those two weeks won't be necessary. Orion is more than capable of taking over immediately."

I have to laugh a little. "That's what I've been saying!"

"Good evening, Emmie."

And he clicks off before I can finish saying, "Merry Christmas, Mr. M."

The kitchen is very quiet. And not in a Silent Night happy sort of way.

Dad is first to speak. "Oh Em."

"I know what I'm doing, Dad."

"I really don't think you do. You're throwing away your future for what? One party?!" He walks out, clearly disappointed in me.

"Dad!"

"Give him a bit of time to digest this," says Mom. "Then talk to him."

I nod. "Mom, I have an idea where Celia might be."

TWENTY-FOUR

The Christmas Wishing Tree is lit so brightly, that it shines and sparkles even in the daylight. Most townspeople must be at home with their families, because when I run up hardly anyone is there. Definitely not Celia, and that's who I'm looking for.

I walk around the tree, looking at all of the little pieces of colorful paper holding the hopes and dreams of the community. I circle the tree, gazing and wondering. What lies in each of them – true love? A teddy bear? A Nintendo Switch? An engagement ring? I circle the tree, wondering what secrets it holds.

And then I see her: Celia sits alone on a bench, quite removed from the tree but gazing up at its beauty.

"Hey."

She doesn't take her eyes off the tree as she replies. "Hey. What are you doing here?"

"Oh, I never put my Christmas wish on the tree. I have until midnight."

Celia looks at me expectantly. I reach in my coat pocket and find a gum wrapper. There's a pencil by the tree, so I use that to write my wish down. I think carefully on what to say, and write down the simple words. I fold up the paper gum wrapper, and give it a kiss for luck.

"No glitter pens? No bedazzling?" asks Celia.

"Not this year. At least the gum wrapper is Wrigley's – so it's green." I place it as I can reach, then go sit by Celia.

"I wouldn't put too much stock in those wishes, Emmie. Turns out they don't always come true."

"What if I told you I had a very special, top-secret message from Santa himself, that your wish was going to come true?"

"Don't, please. It hurts too much."

"Celia, listen to me. I was sworn to secrecy – but it's all been planned. Whit was trying to surprise you."

Celia sits up, the color returning to her face. "What do you mean?"

I shake my head. "I am not going to say anymore. Except for this: trust me."

"Of course I trust you. But how? When?"

"All will be revealed. We have to be somewhere tonight. Right now, it's time for our makeover montage."

Celia smiles. "The best part of every movie. *Clueless*?"

"*The Princess Diaries* for the win."

"No no, it's definitely *The Devil Wears Prada.*"

I give Celia a big smile. "Okay, you win. Now come on."

"Wait," she says. "Don't play with me. My heart can't take it."

I grab her hands in mine. "Whit loves you so much, Celia. All the activities this week were things he asked me and Archer to plan, to make it special for you."

As the realization washes over her, Celia reaches out and hugs me, laughter erupting through her tears.

* * *

Even from the outside, it seems the library has more decorations than ever. Of course, Celia doesn't know that because I'm leading her blindfolded up to the door. She looks absolutely gorgeous, and I'm in a holiday dress myself. As we step inside, I shush all the townspeople who have assembled in their party clothes. Everyone gathers and waits expectantly as I lead Celia to the center of the room and take off her blindfold.

"SURPRISE!"

Celia gasps. "Oh my goodness. Look at all this!" She's overwhelmed with happy emotion. "So many people, everyone is here."

And then I see it – an arbor. It's just like I sketched it,

except it's been built out of books. It's covered with Christmas greenery and twinkle lights, and it really is the perfect centerpiece to the party. I'm beyond touched.

Celia whispers to me, "Where is he?"

I know she means Whit and I don't know where he is, but I have to trust that Archer's going to get him here. "You'll see!" I tell her, faking my confidence.

Meanwhile, Celia says hello and hugs various people including my parents and the young barista and several firefighters and even Kat, who really should be at the party at her own restaurant. Celia spins around taking in all the decorations.

"This is amazing, Em. How did you do it?"

"Archer and I did it together."

"You two make a good team," she says.

And I feel a stab in my heart but I smile. "You look gorgeous, Celia."

Just then, Whit appears. I'm so relieved to see him – but Celia hasn't noticed him yet. The crowd goes quiet as he walks up behind Celia, visibly shaking.

"Celia?"

At the sound of his voice, she freezes. I see the change in the set of her shoulders. Slowly she turns toward him. "Whit, I'm so sorry."

"No, not at all. *I'm* sorry."

The couple walk toward each other, eyes locked, as we all look on – enchanted by their love. I glance around for Archer, wondering where he is.

Whit's voice is shaking as he says, "Celia?"

"Wait!" Celia almost shouts. "I have to say something."

"…Okay."

Everyone in the room is a statue, waiting for what comes next.

With a bold, sweeping movement, Celia goes down on one knee. "Whitman Spence, will you marry me?" She holds out a bit of red ribbon with a jingle bell, the "ring."

I hear gasps and giggles around the room at this unexpected turn of events. I myself am frozen in place, wondering what the answer will be.

Whit's shock quickly turns to a smile. "Yes. Yes, of course yes."

He also goes down on one knee, and from that position, they seal their engagement with a kiss. He whips out another ring, this one with a diamond instead of a jingle bell. I wipe away a happy tear. What a moment. I look around the room at all the beaming faces, but there's still no Archer.

It's an amazing party. Jolly people mingle and eat and celebrate the joyous couple's Christmas engagement. The decorations are on point, the food from Cake My Day is super delicious, and the library was an inspired venue. So why aren't I having more fun?

I find my father, standing alone and eating cookies that Mom brought. "You had to come all the way here just to get one of Mom's peppermint meltaways?"

"Why have something else, when these are the best cookies in town?"

We share a smile. Then I take a deep breath, and dive in.

"Dad, listen. I don't know if I say this enough, but you are my idol. All you've taught me, and your advice – I admire you so much."

He clears his throat, maybe getting a little choked up, but I keep going.

"I appreciate all the opportunities you created for me, but I'm realizing that sometimes instead of following my head, I should follow my heart. And my heart loves…" I look around at the people dancing, party decorations, holiday glee and laughter. "This."

"Em, don't you know – all I want is for you to follow your dreams. I'm here to help you succeed, no matter what you choose. I believe in *you*. Just tell me what direction you're heading, and I'll always be right there cheering you on. And also probably sticking my nose in your business too much. But that comes with the territory when you're a father."

Those words are like a balm to me. We share a father-daughter hug for the ages.

I wipe a tear from my eye. "So, did you eat all the peppermint meltaways, or what?"

"No comment."

POPPY CARTER

* * *

The party is in full swing now, and it's obvious Archer didn't attend. I guess he got all the research he needed, and besides he's probably home finishing up his manuscript. That's fine with me. I am still going to have a good time. I get out on the dance floor with Whit and Celia, bopping to a fast song and celebrating. There's a very cute, happy, lovey-dovey couple dancing right next to us.

The guy dances kind of close to me, and whispers. "Hey, do you think you could plan one of these proposal parties for us too? I want to surprise my girlfriend."

"Of course!" My heart soars. Maybe, just maybe, following my dream will work out.

Celia winks at me. She's always had my back. And I have a feeling she'll be sending more clients my way as well. Who knows, maybe I'll even move back to North Haven. Now that I'm re-starting my life, anything is possible.

Suddenly the lights dim a bit, and the music goes more romantic. Whit and Celia pair off to slow dance. I thread my way off the dance floor, smiling at the sight of so many happy couples. Then something lights up, making me turn around.

Lights have been strung around a big sign that says, *There's Always Something to Look Forward To*. I turn and scan the crowd – and there is Archer, in the back of the room, having just turned the spotlight onto the sign.

We move toward each other. I'm not even aware I'm walking, but I feel the force of Archer drawing me in. We meet in the middle of the dance floor, under the sparkling lights. He takes me into his arms lightly, and we slow dance.

"I like the arbor."

"It was all my idea," he says.

He spins me gently, and when he pulls me back into him, it is much closer.

"You look beautiful. I'm sorry I'm late."

"You missed the proposal."

"I had my own engagement. Get it?"

"I got it. What was it?"

"A date with my book. I finished it."

I still feel a hurt spot around him using me for research, but I try to smile.

"Listen to me, Em. This was absolutely not what Maude said. She had it all wrong. I started out doing this to help Whit, because he wanted his voice to be heard. And after I met you, it was *then* that I got the idea to put in a party planning character. You see?"

"No, not really. What are you saying?"

"I'm saying I didn't hang out with you in order to research the book. What happened is I met you and I got inspired! I started to have feelings that I've never had before, never in my whole life. And I realized I wanted to write about someone who has the capacity for joy and celebration that you have. Someone who wants to celebrate life. It wasn't research. You inspired me to finish the book because of…the feelings I have for you."

"Okay…" For some reason I still am not sure if this is okay with me.

"Listen." He pulls a scrap of paper out of pocket. "This is the last line of the book." He stops dancing and takes a deep breath. I can see it's not easy for him to read this aloud.

"'And in the end, he found the only way to live again was to love again. And to love meant to believe in the future. And to plan for it. He had finally found something to look forward to.'" He looks in my eyes. "The End."

I am getting emotional, but I try to cover. "I'm not sure Maude will like it."

He laughs. "All I care about is what you think."

"I love it."

He pulls me tight, and puts his hand on my cheek, guiding my face gently towards his.

"Archer? I just hope the character keeps it impromptu and spontaneous too. Not everything can be planned."

And with that, Archer dips me. Way deep, like practically a back bend!

I have to laugh. He swoops me back upright effortlessly. I wrap my arms around his neck.

"Archer Mendez, I think you just wrote yourself a happily ever after."

Not able to wait one moment longer, Archer kisses me. And I mean *kisses* me.

No amount of planning could have prepared me for the way it makes me feel.

The next stand-alone short novel in
A Heartfelt Romantic Comedy Series:

Order now!